MIDDLE OF THE NIGHT

MIDDLE OF THE NIGHT

Photographs by courtesy of Slim Aarons

To Sue

MIDDLE OF THE NIGHT *was first presented by Joshua Logan at the ANTA Theatre, New York City, on February 8, 1956, with the following cast:*

(In Order of Appearance)

THE GIRL	Gena Rowlands
THE MOTHER	June Walker
THE KID SISTER	Joan Chambers
THE MANUFACTURER	Edward G. Robinson
THE SISTER	Nancy R. Pollock
THE WIDOW	Betty Walker
THE DAUGHTER	Patricia Benoit
THE CANASTA PLAYER	Ruth Masters
THE NEIGHBOR	Effie Afton
THE FRIEND	Janet Ward
THE SON-IN-LAW	Martin Balsam
THE HUSBAND	Lee Philips

Directed by Joshua Logan
Settings and Lighting by Jo Mielziner
Costumes by Motley

The action of the play takes place in the West Eighties, New York City, between November and February of the present year.

There are three acts.

ACT ONE

ACT ONE

SCENE I

The living room, a bedroom, and a foyer of a four and a half room apartment in the West Eighties. Furnished in lower-middle-class, not much above shabby. We also see the tiled landing outside the apartment, with its iron-railinged stairways leading from the floor below to the floor above.

It is eight-thirty in the morning. The apartment is dark, however, almost murky, as if all the shades were drawn—which they are. For a moment, the thick silence of sleep fills the stage. There is a figure sleeping on the bed in the bedroom, and another figure sleeping on the couch in the living room. We know they are girls from the articles of clothing lying about in each room.

After a long moment, THE GIRL on the couch in the living room sits up, slowly moving her legs till they dangle over the side of the couch. We see now that she is a pretty, blond girl of twenty-five. She is wearing a slip. Her face is swollen and sodden, and she sits heavily, her shoulders slumped. Suddenly she begins to cry. We cannot hear her at first, but we can see the shivering of her shoulders. She stands up and pads aimlessly around the living room, her eyes open, crying more audibly now. Then, as quickly as it began, the abrupt flush

3

*of tears stops, and she sits in the soft chair of the room, her
breath coming in long, shuddering sighs, which eventually
stop. She sits quietly now, her hands folded slackly in her lap.*

*Now she rises, goes to the end table at the side of the
couch, picks up her wrist watch and looks at the time. She
stands frowning as if it were difficult to concentrate on the
reality of the moment, and then she shuffles to the soft chair
again, perches on the edge of it, picks up the telephone receiver at her elbow and dials a number. She waits.*

*There is some movement upstage in the foyer, and then a
woman in her late forties—tall, angular, wearing a blue ki-
mono over her slip and with her hair still early-morning awry
—comes into the bedroom and moves down to the figure of
the girl sleeping on the bed.*

THE GIRL

(*On phone, in living room*)
Hello, who's this—Caroline? Caroline, this is Betty—Betty
Preiss. I just called in to say I won't be in to work today. . . .
No, no, it's nothing like that, it's a personal matter. . . .

THE MOTHER

(*Shaking the blanketed hip on the bed*)
Come on, get up because it's half-past eight.
(THE MOTHER *disappears back into the foyer.*)

THE GIRL

(*On phone*)
The only thing is, I just remembered I took some sales slips
home with me yesterday. . . . I don't know. I think these are

4

the sales slips Mr. Ellman sent down from the factory in Brooklyn yesterday. . . . No, I don't have them on me, Caroline. I left them home. Wait a minute. Yes, I do. I have them in my purse. (THE MOTHER *appears in the living-room doorway, pauses to listen for a moment, then disappears again back into the foyer. In the bedroom,* THE KID SISTER *slowly crawls out from under her blankets during* THE GIRL's *phone call.* THE KID SISTER *is an amiable, if still sluggish, girl of seventeen, wearing rumpled blue pajamas.* THE GIRL *sits huddled on the soft chair in the living room, her eyes closed, the effort of speaking an enormous one*) No, I'm at my mother's house, 120 West Eighty-first Street, apartment 6E. E like in easy. It's on the top floor. . . . All right, you'd better tell Mr. Kingsley about the sales slips. . . . That's really very sweet of you but I'll be in tomorrow. . . . All right, I'll see you. Thank you, Caroline. Good-bye.

(*She seems terribly weary. She rests her head on the palm of her free hand.* THE MOTHER *comes padding into the living room.*)

THE MOTHER

Did you just call in to say you wasn't going to work today? I think you should go in to work, keep your mind occupied. I'm getting dressed, I'm going in to work myself. And Alice'll be in school all day because I'm not up at the Seventy-ninth Street Hanscom's any more. They switched me down to the Fifty-seventh Street bakery, and you'll be here all alone. (*To* THE KID SISTER, *who has appeared in the bedroom doorway*) Will you get dressed and go to school!

(THE KID SISTER *promptly disappears back into her bedroom.*)

THE GIRL

Ma, stay with me a couple of minutes because I feel lousy.

THE MOTHER

Betty, I have a seventeen-year-old daughter still in high school I have to support—

> (THE MOTHER *scowls at her fingers, and a silence falls between the two women.* THE GIRL *finds the silence unbearable.*)

THE GIRL

George and I are not getting along. Listen, I wouldn't have come over here and bothered you with my problems, but I was in a panic last night about two o'clock in the morning. When I got down into the street there were a couple of tough-looking kids hanging on the corner, so I didn't know where to go so I just came up here. Ma, stay with me for about half an hour. I feel lousy.

THE MOTHER

Well, what do you want to say, Betty?

THE GIRL

(*Sits on the edge of the bed*)

George and I, I think our marriage is through. Ma, we have a physical marriage, and that's it. That's the only time he wants me. The rest of the day he's always trying to get away from me. He's got this job with a band in Las Vegas. He's leaving Monday. He came in yesterday and he said, "Listen, want to go out to Las Vegas with me?" The next minute he said, "Maybe you better not come because you won't have any fun out there, it's just a desert. You'll be by yourself all the time. I'll be playing with the band all day." Do you understand what I mean, Ma? He asked me to go because he felt it was his duty as my husband, but he really didn't want me to. He really doesn't like to be with me. Then around eight o'clock I asked him if we could stay home alone that evening. So about five minutes later he said, "Let's go to a movie." That's his idea of being alone with me. You see, we can sit in a movie and he doesn't have to deal with me. He avoids me all the time. So we didn't go to a movie. We watched TV the whole night. I don't think we said a word. Ma, it's not just last night. It's every night. Then I went to bed. Then he came in around one o'clock. He got undressed and got in bed. I turned over to him and I said, "George, just hold me in your arms a little," and he reached over and began feeling my leg. I just wanted him to hold me and talk to me. You know what he was thinking? He just wanted to get me to sleep so I wouldn't bother him any more. So I waited until he was asleep, and I got up and came over here.

THE MOTHER

(*After a moment*)
You get along in bed all right?

THE GIRL

Ma, I just told you. We get along fine that way.

THE MOTHER

Because that's the whole thing, how you get along in bed.
(*Having shown this maternal concern*, THE MOTHER *pauses.*)

7

THE GIRL

I think I want a divorce.

THE MOTHER

Oh, for God's sakes.

THE GIRL

I've been thinking about it for a couple of months.

THE MOTHER

You had a fight with your husband, for heaven's sakes. You'll be kissing and making up before— How long you been married, one year, for heaven's sakes? Stop acting like a baby, will you? Divorce! (*She starts to go, but some suspicion of inadequacy holds her*) Well, Betty, I've got a seventeen-year-old daughter still in high school I've got to support. Your father abandoned me with two little girls on my hands, one of them one year old. I had no source of income. I have scrubbed floors for my two daughters. As heaven is my witness, I have gone down on my knees and scrubbed floors so my two children could eat. I can say now that my two girls are decent girls who have never been in any trouble.

THE GIRL

(*Muttering*)

I'm in trouble now, Ma.

THE MOTHER

Well, as long as you get along in bed, that's the whole thing.
(THE GIRL *turns, and, for lack of anything better to do,
she looks on the end table for her cigarettes.*)

THE GIRL

Well, you better get to work, Ma.

THE MOTHER

Yeah, I'd better get to work because I'm not working up at
the Seventy-ninth Street Hanscom's any more. They switched
me down to the Fifty-seventh Street bakery. I'm working
mornings now. (*Stands, looks at her daughter, aware that
something more is expected of her*) How do you feel? Do you
feel all right?

THE GIRL

I'm fine, Ma. You go to work.

THE MOTHER

All right, so I'm going to get dressed.
(*She shuffles out of the room, turns left at the foyer and
exits.* THE GIRL *sits on the couch, frowning down at the
floor. The scene is held for a moment.*)

The lights fade quickly

SCENE 2

*The lights come up instantly on a room in another apart-
ment. This is a considerably posher living room—what might
be described as West End Avenue elegance. It is one of those
dropped living rooms, separated from the anteroom by two
steps and a wrought-iron railing. Wall-to-wall carpeting,
French Provincial furniture. We can see the front door of the
apartment, leading upstage. The sun streams boldly in through
the windows.*

*The lights are no sooner on than the door to the apartment
opens, and a middle-aged man in his early fifties comes in. He
is warmly bundled up in a winter overcoat and wears a gray
fedora. He is given a little to portliness, but is not an unhand-
some man. He puts away the key he has just used to open the
door. He lets the door close behind him, and, unbuttoning his
coat, he moves across the small anteroom, down the two steps
into the living room, and goes to the telephone, which rests on
a small telephone table beside a straight-back French Provincial
chair. He picks up the receiver, dials, his face expressionless, his
mind occupied with his thoughts. He pushes his hat back a
little as he waits for someone to answer.*

THE MANUFACTURER

(*On phone*)
Hello, Sylvia, this is Mr. Kingsley. I want you to go into my
office, you'll find a piece of paper on my desk with Betty Preiss's

name on it, and an address. . . . No, no, she's at her mother's house, Eighty-fifth Street somewheres. Somebody died in her family or something. . . . Ask Caroline. She knows where it is. No, don't send the boy. I'll pick them up on the way to the factory. It's right in the neighborhood.

(*He looks up at the entrance of two middle-aged women, who have come in from an unseen recess of the apartment. They are West End Avenue women, well dressed but somehow vaguely new-rich. The handsomer of the two is* THE SISTER. *The shorter, stouter and more amiable is* THE WOMAN.)

THE SISTER

What are you doing home so early?

THE MANUFACTURER

(*Still holding the phone, waiting*)
I just stopped in for a minute. I'm going out to the factory. I want to change my shirt. I got some dye on it.

THE SISTER

(*To* THE WOMAN)
Rosalind, you know my brother Jerry?

THE WOMAN

Sure, sure, how are you there?

THE MANUFACTURER

How do you do? (*To his sister, indicating the rest of the apartment with his head*) What's going on in there, the card players?

THE SISTER

(*Stepping down into the living room*)
Yeah, we're playing a little cards. Your daughter Lillian is here with the baby.

THE MANUFACTURER

(*Smiling*)
Oh, yeah? With the baby?

THE SISTER

She dropped in about an hour ago. She drove in to shop a little, so she dropped up here. She wants us to come out to New Rochelle tonight for dinner.

THE MANUFACTURER

Well, I'll tell you, Evelyn, I'm a little tired, and I got to go to Brooklyn yet, and . . .

THE WOMAN

(*Stepping down into the living room*)
Mr. Kingsley, I just want to tell you, you have a lovely apartment here. I was away in Europe, my married daughter

12

and myself, for three months, we had a wonderful time, so this is my first time in this apartment, and as I was telling your sister, it's just beautiful. How much rent do you pay, if I may ask?

THE MANUFACTURER

Two hundred and forty.

THE WOMAN

I was in your other apartment once when you lived on Central Park West. I don't know whether you recall me or not. My name is Mrs. Nieman.

THE MANUFACTURER

How do you do?

THE WOMAN

I knew your wife casually. She was a lovely woman, and I was distressed at the news. We were in Bermuda at the time, we had a wonderful time, and Mrs. Hillman, I don't know if you knew her but she was a close friend of your wife's, called me on the phone and told me of her passing, and I wondered whether I should send some kind of greeting, but I felt we were not that well acquainted, so I would like to take this opportunity, belated as it is—it's more than a year now, isn't it?— to express my sympathy and condolences.

THE MANUFACTURER

Thank you. Well, listen, don't let me hold you from your game.

THE SISTER

I just got up to make coffee, anyway. Would you like a cup?

THE MANUFACTURER

Yeah, make me a cup. (*His attention is called back to the phone*) Yeah, that's right, yeah. . . . All right, let me get a pencil. . . . (*He fishes in his jacket pocket and extracts a pencil and an envelope.*)

THE SISTER

(*To* THE WOMAN)

Stay here, it'll take me a minute.
(THE WOMAN *looks at her, undecided for a moment, but* THE SISTER *turns and moves out up through the anteroom and disappears into the recesses of the apartment.*)

THE MANUFACTURER

(*On phone*)

All right, so listen, Sylvia. I'm going out to the factory from here. I'll be there about half-past three. If Lockman calls, tell him I went out to the factory, I'm getting the samples, I'll have the boy bring them down the shop, he can pick them up around half-past four. . . . All right. So I won't be in the rest of the day. . . . All right. (*He hangs up, looks up, a little surprised at Mrs. Nieman's presence. He slips out of his coat*) Nieman. I used to know a Nieman, used to supply us with embroideries about seven, eight years ago.

THE WOMAN

That's my brother-in-law, used to be in embroideries.

THE MANUFACTURER

Is that right? A very nice fellow. Whatever happened to him?

THE WOMAN

He moved to Los Angeles.

THE MANUFACTURER

Oh, yeah, that's right.

THE WOMAN

He's in the hospital now. Gall bladder. Nothing serious. We thought for a while he had to have an operation, but he's responding to treatment beautifully.

THE MANUFACTURER

Well, listen, you get to our age, you figure a couple of weeks in the hospital every year.

THE WOMAN

Absolutely.

THE MANUFACTURER

These are the years, you know. Everybody starts dropping dead around you. A man I know for twenty years, I played cards with him every Wednesday for years—he died last week in the hospital. Cancer.

THE WOMAN

Perhaps you know Roger Benedict. He used to live in this neighborhood. His wife was president of the PTA here in Public School 9 for many years.

THE MANUFACTURER

I'm afraid I don't know him.

THE WOMAN

He died last month. A cerebral hemorrhage. A relatively young man. Fifty-eight. Far from old.

THE MANUFACTURER

My wife was only forty-eight when she died.

THE WOMAN

My own husband passed away only last July.

THE MANUFACTURER

(*Glances quickly at* THE WOMAN, *suddenly wary*)
I'm very sorry to hear that.

THE WOMAN

I have a twenty-eight-year-old son. I live with him, and my married daughter is very solicitous. They took me, she and her husband, for three months in Europe, we had a wonderful time. He works for a chemical concern, very successful. But it's very difficult to give up a companionship of so many years.

THE MANUFACTURER

Well, it's a very lonely business. There's no doubt about it. But you get used to it.

THE WOMAN

Well, I must admit I'm very lonely.

THE MANUFACTURER

Well, if you'll excuse me, Mrs. Nieman, I have to change my shirt.

(THE MANUFACTURER *goes up into the anteroom to greet a young woman who has just entered. She is twenty-five, big-boned but handsome, amiable and smiling, and carries a blanketed baby. She is followed by* THE SISTER, *who is carrying a cup and saucer.*)

THE DAUGHTER

Hello, Pa, how are you?

THE MANUFACTURER

(*With open-armed welcome*)
Well, for God's sakes, what did you do, drive all the way in with the baby?

(THE SISTER *steps into the living room and sets the coffee on the telephone table.*)

17

THE SISTER

Jerry, I'm putting your coffee here.

THE MANUFACTURER

(*To his daughter*)

How are you, sweetheart? What did you do, just feed him?
Look how he's sleeping.

THE SISTER

(*To* THE WOMAN)

Rosalind, do me a favor. The coffee is all ready. Pour in the
cups and take it in on the tray there where the cake is . . .

THE MANUFACTURER

(*To his daughter*)

Let me hold him. . . .

THE SISTER

(*To* THE WOMAN)

Also, there's some petit fours in the refrigerator . . .

THE DAUGHTER

(*Giving the baby to her father*)

So how's everything, Pa? Put the cigar down, Pa. . . .

THE MANUFACTURER

Fine . . .

THE SISTER

(*To* THE WOMAN)

. . . and you know where I put the serving plate with the doily on it . . .

THE WOMAN

. . . Sure, sure . . .

THE MANUFACTURER

(*Moving back into the living room with the baby*)

. . . Boy, you're getting heavy, kid. You're going to weigh like a bolt of cloth pretty soon. . . .

THE WOMAN

(*To* THE SISTER)

. . . You want me to serve the coffee?

THE SISTER

. . . Would you, please, Rosalind? I'll be right in.

THE MANUFACTURER

(*Sitting down with the baby*)

. . . So what's new, Lillian?

THE DAUGHTER

(*Moving down into the living room*)

. . . Nothing. Same old story. . . .

THE SISTER

So, Rosalind, would you take it in because the coffee is perked all ready.

THE WOMAN

Sure. So, Mr. Kingsley, it was wonderful to have made your acquaintance.

THE MANUFACTURER

Very nice to have met you, Mrs. Nieman.

THE WOMAN

Some time, when your sister drops over for a visit, why don't you come along?

THE MANUFACTURER

Absolutely, Mrs. Nieman. Very nice of you to invite me.
(THE WOMAN *steps into the anteroom, smiling at* THE DAUGHTER, *who smiles back pleasantly.*)

THE SISTER

I'll be in in a minute, Rosalind. Pour six cups. (THE WOMAN *nods, smiles and exits*) A very nice woman, really. Her husband died just about a half-year ago, left her quite an estate. A well-educated woman and very sweet, really.

THE MANUFACTURER

(*Rather brusquely*)
Don't matchmake, Evelyn. I don't like it.

THE SISTER

What are you talking about? Did I know you were coming home three o'clock in the afternoon?

THE MANUFACTURER

No, you didn't know, but, if I had come home at the regular time, she would have been here just the same.

THE DAUGHTER

Is she trying to marry you off, Pa?

THE SISTER

He sits around the house, for God's sakes, every night. He comes home, he eats dinner, he goes to sleep.

THE MANUFACTURER

I work hard, and I'm tired, and I come home, and I . . .

THE SISTER

Helen died, it's almost two years now. It's time to stop mourning, Jerry.

THE MANUFACTURER

I'm not mourning. Stop making a soap opera out of this. Now, I want an end to this business, Evelyn. Is that clear? I'm very annoyed by this.

(*He frowns angrily down at the baby in his arms. His sister and daughter stand a moment in silent discomfort.*)

THE SISTER

So, do you want to go up to Lillian's tonight or not?

THE MANUFACTURER

(*Angrily*)

I said no, didn't I?

THE SISTER

(*Looks down at the floor, shrugs*)
I can see you're in a bad temper.
(*She turns and goes up the steps into the anteroom.*)

THE DAUGHTER

I'll be in in a little while, Evelyn. I just want to put the baby
to sleep. I'll put him on your bed, all right?

THE SISTER

Sure, nobody will bother him.
(*She exits off into the apartment.* THE MANUFACTURER
turns back to the baby, regaining his usual good humor.)

THE MANUFACTURER

(*Without looking up*)
I'll tell you something, Lillian. I think I'm going through a
change of life.

THE DAUGHTER

Yeah?

THE MANUFACTURER

(*Looks up, smiling*)

Yeah. I've become very touchy lately. I lose my temper any little thing. You should have seen me screaming at a salesman this morning. Listen, men go through a change of life too. (*Apparently the baby stirs in his arms, because he hastens to quiet it with tender solicitude, standing as he does*) Stevie, Stevie boy, we woke you up. Oh, he's a sweetheart. (THE DAUGH-TER *sits comfortably back into a soft chair*) A friend of mine named Louie Sherman, you know him, he used to come up when we used to live on Central Park West, play cards all the time.

THE DAUGHTER

Sure, I know Mr. Sherman.

THE MANUFACTURER

Well, he's retiring from his business. He was up the office today, his doctor told him he has very low blood pressure. If you remember, he once fainted in our house. Anyway, he's retiring. It seems to me everybody's dying, everybody's in the hospital, everybody's retiring. Listen, when you get to fifty, fifty-five, believe me . . . I'll be sitting in the shop there, cutting a pattern, when suddenly, for no reason, I'll think, "My God, I'm fifty-three years old. I'll be an old man with white hair soon. My life is coming to an end." Listen, I know it sounds very irrational, but listen . . .

THE DAUGHTER

No, Pa, I can understand how you feel.

23

THE MANUFACTURER

You're a good kid, Lillian. I look at you, and I say to my-self, "I didn't do so bad if I have a couple of mature, grown-up kids like you and Paul."

THE DAUGHTER

Pa, why don't you come up to dinner tonight?

THE MANUFACTURER

Well, we was up to your house Monday, and we was there Thursday before. (*He suddenly concerns himself with the baby in his arms*) Listen, you better take him. He's getting restless.

THE DAUGHTER

Just put him on the couch, Pa. He'll fall asleep.
(THE MANUFACTURER *lays the blanketed baby down on the couch.*)

THE MANUFACTURER

I better get a shirt, it's getting late. I got to go out to Brooklyn. Lockman is taking out a buyer tonight, and the samples are still out in the factory, and I better get out there.

THE DAUGHTER

Sit down a minute, Pa. Let's talk a minute.

THE MANUFACTURER

(*Frowning*)
Well, Lillian, I'm going through a kind of period—a change of life, it's the best way I can describe it— It's a transitional

24

thing. I've seen my friends go through it. Listen, you met Walter Lockman, one of my partners. He's going through hell. He's a man fifty-nine, going to be sixty, and, in the last couple of years, he has become absolutely obsessed with women. That's all he talks about. He comes in the office, the first thing he says, he's got a story about some girl he was out with. It's always a beautiful girl, and it always winds up the girl tells him that he's a better lover than all the young men she knows. And he sees doctors. Pills, everything. If it wasn't so sad, it would be comic. And listen, this is a man with four grown children, a grandfather three times. Walter, I'll tell you quite frankly, I'm worried about. But with me, it's a sort of vaguely depressed state. Your mother went through the same thing. In fact, I recognize many symptoms about myself. Look, don't let me bother you with all this, because you don't understand it, and you'll make more out of it than it really is.

THE DAUGHTER

Evelyn tells me that you sit sometimes in the living room like a corpse.

THE MANUFACTURER

Evelyn. You don't know by now not to listen to Evelyn.

THE DAUGHTER

Pa, how's your sex life?

(THE MANUFACTURER *regards his daughter for a moment. Then laughs gently.*)

THE MANUFACTURER

(*Ruffling his daughter's hair*)
You're all right, Lillian.

THE DAUGHTER

I'm serious, Pa. You're a vigorous man with normal appetites.

THE MANUFACTURER

(*Smiling at her*)
You're funny. All right, my sex life is not so hot.

THE DAUGHTER

I meant it very seriously.

THE MANUFACTURER

I know you did, sweetheart. I know a woman. I go up to see her every now and then. A nice woman. A widow. She's a buyer for a department store. Lord and Taylor's, if you want to know. She's a very tasteful woman, quite attractive, her early forties. (*He turns away, somehow disturbed by this confession*) Actually, I haven't seen her in a couple of months now. If you want to know, I asked her to marry me, and she said no, and I was very hurt, actually. (*He turns back to his daughter*) For God's sakes, what am I telling you all this nonsense for?

THE DAUGHTER

Don't be silly, Pa. You got to pour out your heart to somebody.

THE MANUFACTURER

No, no, I'm putting you in a terrible position. You're not my wife. I'm going through a kind of temporary depression. It'll pass in time—a month, two months. Don't worry about it.

(THE SISTER *appears in the anteroom. She is carrying a man's white shirt.*)

THE SISTER

Lillian, don't you want some coffee?

THE MANUFACTURER

Go ahead, Lillian, go have your coffee.

THE SISTER

(*Coming down into the living room*)
I brought you a new shirt, Jerry. Mrs. Mason feels a little sick, she's lying down on your bed, so you change in here. Nobody'll come in.

THE MANUFACTURER

All right.
(*He unbuttons his double-breasted jacket.*)

THE DAUGHTER

(*Picking up the baby*)
All right, Pa, so when'll we see you?

THE MANUFACTURER

We'll be up some time next week.

THE DAUGHTER

(*Moving to the anteroom*)
Listen, Evelyn, I'll put him on your bed.

THE SISTER

Fine.

THE DAUGHTER

All right, Pa, come in and say good-bye before you go.

THE MANUFACTURER

(*Now unbuttoning a noticeably stained shirt*)
I'll come in.

(THE DAUGHTER *exits.* THE SISTER *moves down into the
living room, puts the shirt on a chair. She looks briefly
at her brother, who is expressionlessly taking off his
shirt. Then she looks out the window.*)

THE SISTER

You want to eat in a restaurant tonight, because I really
haven't got anything in the house?

THE MANUFACTURER

Fine.

THE SISTER

I was going to go shopping this morning, but I woke up with
a headache and before I knew it the girls were here for
canasta, and I never had a chance even to phone down an
order.

THE MANUFACTURER

Fine, we'll eat out.

(*He picks up the fresh shirt, removes the cardboard and
collar bracing.*)

THE SISTER

You want to go to a movie tonight?

THE MANUFACTURER

(*Unbuttoning the fresh shirt*)
I'm a little tired. Why don't you call one of your friends, go to a movie with her?

THE SISTER

(*Makes a wry face*)
Tell you the truth, I got a little headache. Maybe we'll take a little walk after dinner. (*She looks at him quickly, a little apprehensively*) Well, listen, maybe, if you don't want to see Lillian, maybe we'll drive down and see Paul and his . . .

THE MANUFACTURER

(*Whirls on her in a fury, crying out*)
Evelyn, I don't want to visit my children! I hope to God I haven't reached that point where I don't know what to do with myself, I have to go visit my children!

THE SISTER

(*Sensitive to the presence of her friends in the other room*)
All right, all right . . .

THE MANUFACTURER

(*Walking around the room furiously*)
God Almighty, you can drive somebody right out of their minds! How many times . . .

THE SISTER

All right, all right . . .

THE MANUFACTURER

. . . do I have to tell you I don't want to visit my children! I'm tired, for God's sakes! I'm fifty-three years old! Will you get that in your mind, God Almighty! I do a hard day's work! I come home! I want to watch a little TV, go to sleep! Stop trying to marry me off! Stop trying to fix me up with all your friends! I'm fifty-three years old! (*Another middle-aged woman, obviously attracted by the loud voices, suddenly pokes her head into the anteroom.* THE SISTER *looks quickly at her and embarrassedly back. The woman promptly disappears.* THE MANUFACTURER *angrily puts on his fresh shirt, buttons it, breathing heavily. After a moment, he mutters*) Evelyn, I'm a little depressed and angry today. It would be a good policy for you to stay away from me.

THE SISTER

All right, I'll leave you alone. (*She stands a moment, then turns and goes up the steps to the anteroom, where she pauses*) So you'll be home around six?

THE MANUFACTURER

Yeah. (THE SISTER *nods involuntarily, exits off into the apartment.* THE MANUFACTURER *finishes buttoning his shirt, his face a dark scowl, his mind tumbling with dark thoughts. He sits down on the soft chair, with his shirt tails still out. He sits for a moment, his face set and troubled. Then, pulling himself together, he stands, stuffs his shirt into his trousers, takes his tie, adjusts it into his collar. He pauses abruptly and stands rigidly as some troubled thoughts lurch through his mind. He moves*

to the telephone, sits down on the straight-back French Pro-
vincial chair, picks up the receiver, dials Information, waits,
fixing his tie as he sits. Then, on phone) Can you give me the
telephone number of Lord and Taylor Department Store? . . .
Yes, thank you. . . . *(He waits again, cradling the receiver on*
his shoulder so that his two hands are left free to tie his necktie
knot. In the middle of tying it, his attention is called back
to the phone) Yes . . . Yes, thank you. . . . *(He pushes the*
receiver holder down, then dials again, his face assuming a
determined, expressionless cast. He finishes tying his necktie
knot as he waits) Hello, Lord and Taylor's? Infants' wear department, please. . . . *(He just sits now, waiting)* Hello, is
Miss Herbert there? . . . Miss Herbert, the buyer? . . . Could
you switch me, please? *(The tension of the phone call is be-*
ginning to tell on him now. Apparently he is sweating, for he
wipes his brow quickly with his fingers. Then he adjusts a
smile onto his face and nails it there) Hello, Grace? This is
Jerry Kingsley, how are you, for God's sakes? . . . Yeah, Jerry
Kingsley. Listen, are you busy or can you spare me a few
minutes? . . . No, no, nothing important. I just called, it's
been how many months now? Frankly, I'd like to see you. . . .
(He moves the receiver quickly away from his mouth and
takes a deep, shuddering breath) Oh, is that right, when are
you leaving? . . . Well, listen, there's a whole week end. How
about tonight? We'll have a little dinner, maybe we'll take in a
show. . . . *(The hearty smile remains plastered on his face,*
but he has closed his eyes, and the pain of the call is evident)
Are you angry with me, Grace, because you seem so un-
friendly? . . . Oh, really? Well, I didn't know that, of course.
Congratulations. Do I know the man? . . . Well, that's wonderful, Grace. I hope from the bottom of my heart that you'll
be very happy because you're a good woman. . . . Well, he's a

31

very lucky fellow, whoever he is. . . . Of course, dear. . . . No, no, don't let me hold you up from your work. You must be terribly busy with the season starting and . . . Of course. My very best wishes to you and your future husband. . . . Of course, good-bye. . . . (*He hangs up. For a moment, he sits. Then he stands. A sort of pensiveness has come over him. He looks absently around the room for his jacket, finds it on a chair, picks it up, puts it on, buttons it, adjusts it. He picks up his coat, drapes it over his arm, picks up his gray fedora. He moves up the steps into the anteroom, turns to look down the foyer leading to the unseen parts of the apartment. Apparently he sees someone. A vague, tenuous smile slips onto his lips, and he calls down the foyer*) Lillian. . . . (*He moves a step toward the foyer*) Lillian, sweetheart . . . no, no, stay there. Listen, sweetheart, I'll tell you what. It's a little after three now. Why don't you stick around? I'll be back around six, and, what the hell, we'll drive out to New Rochelle, have dinner with you.

THE DAUGHTER

(*Off stage*)

That's wonderful, Pa.

THE MANUFACTURER

All right, then? So I'll be back as soon as I can. So tell Evelyn.

(*He turns abruptly, puts his hat on, moves quickly to the front door, putting on his coat as he goes. He opens the door, and exits, still slipping into his coat. The door closes with a soft click.*)

The lights fade quickly

SCENE 3

The lights come up in THE GIRL'S *apartment. It is three-thirty in the afternoon. The Venetian blinds in* THE KID SISTER'S *bedroom have been opened, and fierce sunlight streams into that room. Indeed, although none of the beds have been made, and the clothes are still strewn about as they were in Scene 1, the whole apartment is bright with the light of the afternoon sun.*

A young girl comes hurrying down the stairs from the floor above and disappears down to the floor below. Then, for a moment, the stage is silent. There is a movement in the foyer now, and THE GIRL *strides nervously into the living room. She is wearing the black dress that had been draped over the back of a chair in Scene 1, and she has combed her blond hair. She is a strikingly pretty girl. She seems, however, to be governed by an enormous restlessness. Frowning, she moves around the living room, holding a glass ash tray in one hand, into which she continuously flicks the cigarette she is smoking. With a deep sigh, she sits down on the soft chair by the telephone, and then, cigarette in mouth, lifts the telephone receiver as if she is going to dial, but changes her mind, and sets the phone down again. She rises, and, still carrying the ash tray, goes to the unmade couch, lies down, setting the ash tray on the floor beside her, tapping her cigarette nervously into it. A moment later she gets up again, crosses to the phone, lifts the receiver and starts to dial, standing beside the telephone table. She waits for an answer. Apparently somebody finally does answer. Her eyes suddenly close, and she almost cries at her success.*

33

THE GIRL

(On phone)

Where have you been, for God's sakes, Marilyn? This is Betty. I must have called you twenty times. . . . Betty Preiss, for God's sakes. . . . Yes, yes. I called you around eleven. I called you every half-hour on the half-hour. It's twenty minutes after three now. . . . Well, you couldn't have been taking a shower all that time. . . . Well, how's Frank and the kids? . . . No, I'm at my mother's house. . . . Well, who told you? . . . Oh, really, when was this? . . . You mean, he called you four o'clock in the morning? . . . Well, then you know all about it. . . . No, he finally got me. He called here about half-past eight this morning. Listen, Marilyn, can I come over and stay with you for a couple of nights? I'll sleep on the couch. I'm over here at my mother's house, and . . . Well, when will Frank get home? . . . I'm not blaming George, Marilyn. He's a nice guy, but . . . Marilyn, can I come over and see you, because I'm going crazy all alone here? My kid sister called about twenty minutes ago. She won't be home till dinner, and . . . I don't know, Marilyn. I don't want to talk about this over the phone. Can I come over and see you? . . . *(She sinks slowly into the soft chair, her eyes closed, exhausted again)* Can I come over after dinner then? . . . Well, do you have to go see your mother tonight? I need to talk to somebody because . . . Well, how seriously sick is she? . . . Well, give Frank my best . . . No, no, no, it's all right, Marilyn. . . . No, I'm all right, Marilyn. No, it's . . . No, I'll call you late tonight. . . . Sure . . . Okay, I'll see you. *(She hangs up, crushes out her cigarette. Her attention falls on the television set. She pads to the set, turns it on, waits expressionlessly. After the usual moment of station adjustment, the program comes on. It is "The Ted Mack Matinee," a program perhaps best described as a*

*variety show. She stands in front of the set, watching the show
with no expression. Then, with sudden shrill fury)* For God's
sakes! For God's sakes! . . . *(She walks around, feverishly
restless, her arms moving jerkily as she paces. She looks up at
the ceiling again and screams out)* Oh, my God, my God!
*(THE MANUFACTURER appears now, coming up the stairs to the
landing. In the living room, THE GIRL continues to move restlessly, almost bursting with frustration. THE MANUFACTURER lo-
cates the apartment easily enough, rings the bell. The sound of
the bell, which is a raucous buzz, startles THE GIRL. She goes out
into the foyer, turning to her left, and reappears a moment
later, coming down the foyer to answer the door. She opens it,
sees her employer. Trying to control herself)* Hello, Mr. Kingsley, how are you? I didn't expect you personally. I thought they
were going to send the boy up.

THE MANUFACTURER

It was on my way. I live right in the neighborhood.

THE GIRL

Come in for a minute, Mr. Kingsley.

THE MANUFACTURER

Perhaps it would be better if I waited out here.

THE GIRL

There's nobody home, Mr. Kingsley.

THE MANUFACTURER

I was under the impression someone was sick in your family.

35

THE GIRL

No. Please come in. (THE MANUFACTURER *moves tentatively into the foyer.* THE GIRL *has already turned on her heel and is moving with nervous quickness down the foyer.* THE MANUFACTURER *closes the door and follows her slowly.* THE GIRL *reappears in the living room, coming quickly to the telephone table, where her purse is lying. She opens it, takes out a stapled pile of papers, turns toward the living-room door, through which* THE MANUFACTURER *is just now coming*) Please excuse the condition of the room, Mr. Kingsley. Here are the slips, Mr. Kingsley. I hope they're the ones.

THE MANUFACTURER

(*Taking the papers*)
You seem very distraught. Is there something I can do?

THE GIRL

No, no, Mr. Kingsley, no, that's all right. I'm all right. Well, I'll tell you what it is. I had a fight with my husband, and we're breaking up, and I don't know. (*The thin veneer of her control begins to crack. She turns nervously away, trying not to cry*) Oh, I don't know. (*A hoarse, racking sob escapes her now, and she begins to cry with painful and deep agony. The tears stream down her cheeks, and she walks quickly away from her boss, horribly embarrassed. She mumbles*) Excuse me, Mr. Kingsley . . .

THE MANUFACTURER

(*A little ill at ease*)
Don't be silly.

36

THE GIRL

Excuse me . . . (*She sits down on the soft chair and bends forward so that her face is buried in her knees. She sits, hunched into a ball, as if she were in physical pain, unsuccessfully trying not to cry, mumbling between sobs*) I'm sorry, Mr. Kingsley . . .

THE MANUFACTURER

Isn't there somebody home with you here? Your mother or somebody?

(THE GIRL *abruptly stands up again, and, shielding her face with her hand, she walks around the living room.* THE MANUFACTURER *stands, not quite sure what to do.*)

THE GIRL

(*As she walks, mumbling*)
Stay with me a minute, please, Mr. Kingsley.

THE MANUFACTURER

I'm sorry, dear. I didn't hear what you said.

THE GIRL

I said, stay with me a minute, please. I'm sorry about this, Mr. Kingsley.

THE MANUFACTURER

Don't be so embarrassed. Sometimes life gets so complicated, the only thing you can do is scream.

37

THE GIRL

(*In confusion*)

It just burst out of me. I've been calling my friends all day, but none of them are home. It's just one of those days. He's a nice guy, really, my husband. Everybody likes him. He's a piano player. No, he's more than that. He's a pianist. He plays classical as well as jazz. He's very good-looking, by the way. He flirts a lot, but I don't think he ever did anything. That's just one of his little vanities, that he's so attractive, and I don't mind it, really. No, that's not true. I do mind it a lot. But that isn't it, his flirting, I mean. Oh, Mr. Kingsley, you'd better grab those sales slips and escape. Don't let me take advantage of you like this.

THE MANUFACTURER

Please, Betty, don't worry about me.

THE GIRL

You know what my husband would do if he came in like you just did and found me breaking down like I just did, do you know what he'd do? He'd turn on the television set, do you know what I mean, Mr. Kingsley? Or else he'd invite the neighbors in. Anything except sit down with me and talk things out. Oh, I'm not being fair to him. He tried, he really tried. You just can't imagine how naïve I was about marriage, Mr. Kingsley. I really thought you lived happily ever after. Look, Mr. Kingsley, if I sound like I'm blaming my husband, I don't want to sound that way. This is me. I wanted poor George to make up for everything I never had in my life. My father ran away when I was six years old. Oh, Mr. Kingsley, here I go again. You'd better get out of here because I've been building up all day like a volcano.

THE MANUFACTURER

Please don't worry about me.

THE GIRL

(*Suddenly*)

Did you ever go downtown in the afternoon by the Para-mount Theatre? Did you ever see those fourteen- and fifteen-year-old kids hanging around, cutting school? They're the loneliest-looking kids in the world. Well, that's just what I was like when I was a kid. I used to go to the Paramount three or four times a week. I didn't cut school, though. I was always very good in school. Can I get you something to eat or drink, Mr. Kingsley? I don't know what we have in the house. I haven't eaten all day, but do you know what I mean by lonely kids, Mr. Kingsley? (*She begins to cry; she wanders around the room, distracted*)

I'm sorry, Mr. Kingsley, but just seeing you sitting there, listening to me . . . Boy, you came here just to pick up a couple of sales slips. Oh, Mr. Kingsley, I'm so glad you came. My husband, George, the last couple of months we've hardly talked to each other. He comes home and I ask him what hap-pened during the day. He always says, "Nothing." We never eat home any more. We go to a restaurant and we just sit there, eating. He doesn't know what to do with me, do you know what I mean? There's no love or anything. Well, I can't stand that. I want him to love me. I want him to be pleased to see me. I want him to come home and tell me all that's hap-pened to him and how he feels about things. And I want to tell him how I feel. I want something. I mean, is this what marriage is? Is this what life is? Boy, life isn't much if that's what it is. The other night we had this big fight and he came in the next morning . . .

(*The lights dim quickly.* THE GIRL's *voice fades into inaudibility. There is a moment of silence and the stage is completely dark. Then the living-room lamp is turned on, casting a sharp cone of light in the dark room. Through the window of* THE KID SISTER's *room, we can see it is nighttime.* THE MANUFACTURER, *who has just turned on the lamp, has taken his coat off.* THE GIRL *is lying on the couch now, her head propped up against one arm of the couch. She is still talking, as if she had been talking throughout the passage of hours. Now, however, there is a noticeable increase of energy and animation. She is almost gay, exhilarated by her patient, cigar-smoking audience.*)

THE GIRL

. . . So any time we have a fight, that's just what happens. So one time, you know what happened? . . .
(*She sits up quickly, leaning across to her boss, eager to tell another incident. She notices he is looking at his watch.*)

THE MANUFACTURER
(*Smiling*)
You know what time it is?

THE GIRL

Boy, I've been talking your head off.

THE MANUFACTURER

It's half-past six. Do you mind if I use your phone?

THE GIRL

Mr. Kingsley, I'm terribly sorry I used up your afternoon like this.

40

THE MANUFACTURER

Don't be sorry. Do you feel better?

THE GIRL

Oh, I feel much better. (*She stands*) I really do, got this all off my chest. Gee, half-past six. I don't know where my mother and my sister are. My mother's on a new shift now. I don't know what time she gets home. Would you like to stay for dinner, Mr. Kingsley?

THE MANUFACTURER

No, I don't think so, dear. I have to make a call though.

THE GIRL

The phone's right there. (*He reaches for the phone, but before he can pick up the receiver,* THE GIRL *is talking again*) So, what do you think I ought to do? I've been considering a divorce for a couple of months now, but it seems so complicated. I don't know anybody who's divorced, so I don't know how you go about it. My mother, she won't hear about divorce. My grandmother was Catholic. My mother's a Lutheran, but even so. My husband, it would just kill him. His vanity would be so hurt.

(*She sits and stares at the middle-aged, cigar-smoking man in the soft chair.*)

THE MANUFACTURER

Betty, tell me something. How old are you?

THE GIRL

I'll be twenty-four in March.

THE MANUFACTURER

Twenty-four years old. I have a daughter of my own, twenty-five years old, lives out in New Rochelle, she's married now with two fine children, and you make me think of her when she was ten years old. So I'm going to talk to you like I was your father. About twenty times tonight, you've asked me, "What should I do about my husband?" Betty, this is a decision you have to make for yourself. Don't expect your mother to make it for you, or your husband's mother, and don't worry so much about hurting your husband.

THE GIRL

Because I know this would hurt him.

THE MANUFACTURER

The only person you have to worry about hurting is yourself. You have to do what you want to do, not what other people want you to do; otherwise you and everyone else concerned will be miserable. You have to say to yourself, "Do I want to go back to him or do I think I can find something better for my life?"

THE GIRL

I don't want to go back to him.

42

THE MANUFACTURER

All right, there's your decision. (THE GIRL *looks at him, a little confused at the sudden clarity of her situation*) If it means a divorce, then you go ahead and get one. You go to a lawyer, and he'll tell you what you'll have to do. It may be a little complicated, but nothing is too complicated. Then you start going out on dates again, and take my word for it, you'll run across some young fellow who will understand that you need a lot of kindness. There are plenty of nice young fellows around, believe me.

THE GIRL

You know something? I really feel much better now . . .

THE MANUFACTURER

Sure, you do . . .

THE GIRL

. . . talking it out like this.

THE MANUFACTURER

Well, you made a decision, and suddenly there's not such big, black clouds in the sky, and it isn't going to rain, and life isn't so terrible. Life, believe me, can be a beautiful business. And you're a young kid, and you got plenty of joy ahead of you. So go wash your face. I want to make a phone call.

THE GIRL

(*Stands*)

I want to thank you very much, Mr. Kingsley, for letting me pour my heart out.

43

THE MANUFACTURER

There's nothing to thank, sweetheart.

(THE MANUFACTURER *reaches over for the phone and begins to dial.*)

THE GIRL

Your wife must have had a wonderful life with you.

(THE MANUFACTURER *pauses in his dialing to look up at* THE GIRL.)

THE MANUFACTURER

(*Touched*)

That's a very sweet thing for you to say, my dear.

THE GIRL

Well, I'll go wash my face.

(*She turns and goes out into the foyer, disappearing to her right. We see her passing the open doorway of her sister's room.* THE MANUFACTURER *returns to his dialing. He waits, then gets an answer.*)

THE MANUFACTURER

(*On phone*)

Hello, Evelyn, this is Jerry. . . . No, I'll tell you what happened. Is Lillian still there? . . . Well, I see it's half-past six. I tell you, I'm very, very tired right now. Why don't you drive out with Lillian, and I'll catch a bite around the corner, and you can take the train in from New Rochelle tomorrow. . . . Well, I'll tell you. I never got out to Brooklyn. Remember I told about this girl in the office who was sick? . . . I didn't tell you? . . . No, Betty Preiss, the very pretty one. She sits by the reception window. . . . You know her. The very pretty one. So I had to stop off at her house, pick up some papers she had, she didn't come in today. So I come up here, I tell you, this girl was in an emotional state. So, to cut a long story short, I talked to her, it turns out, she's leaving her husband, that's why she couldn't come in today, and it poured out of her, the whole story. . . . No, no, no, the blond girl, the very pretty one. The fat one is Elaine. . . . The exceptionally attractive one. I used to look at her, I used to think, "A beautiful girl like that, what problems could she have? The young men must fall all over themselves." This girl is a real beauty. I've seen lots of girls on television who aren't so beautiful. An intelligent girl, a good worker, but emotionally very immature. . . . (*Annoyed*) Oh, don't be foolish. What did you mean, I'm showing a marked interest in how beautiful she is? It happens that she's a very pretty girl. . . . All right, so you go out to New Rochelle if you want to and . . . I'll tell you the truth, I think I'll just come home and go to bed. . . .

(THE GIRL *returns to the living-room doorway, where she pauses.* THE MANUFACTURER *darts a look at her*)

No, I'll be fine. . . . Apologize to Lillian for me. . . . Absolutely, why should you stay in the house? . . . Fine, give my regards to Jack and the kids. . . . All right, I'll see you.

(*He hangs up, stands, frowning for some unaccountable reason.*)

THE GIRL

I don't know what happened to my family.

(THE MANUFACTURER *has found his coat and is putting it on.*)

THE MANUFACTURER

I'll take the slips here with me.

THE GIRL

I hope I didn't inconvenience you too much, Mr. Kingsley.

THE MANUFACTURER

It was no inconvenience. I was supposed to go out to the factory, but, I tell you, I was grateful to get out of it. I had the boy deliver the stuff. (*He puts on his hat*) I have the feeling you didn't eat anything at all today.

THE GIRL

You know, I really don't think I did.

THE MANUFACTURER

Well, eat something now. (*He starts for the door to the foyer, pauses on the threshold, looks at his watch*) It's almost seven o'clock. (*He frowns*) Listen, you want a bite to eat? Come on, I'll buy you a bite to eat.

(THE GIRL *considers this suggestion with no particular expression.*)

THE GIRL

I'd like to very much, Mr. Kingsley. I have to put some make-up on.

THE MANUFACTURER

Hurry up, put some make-up on.

(THE GIRL *smiles briefly, turns and heads for the foyer door.*)

THE GIRL

(*As she goes*)

I'll just be a minute, Mr. Kingsley.

(*She disappears into the foyer, carrying her purse, which she has picked up on her way out.* THE MANUFACTURER *moves slowly downstage into the living room. He puts his hands into his coat pockets and walks slowly around the room.*)

THE MANUFACTURER

(*Suddenly calling out*)

You like Italian food? Very good restaurant here on Seventy-ninth Street. (*Apparently* THE GIRL *doesn't hear him, for there is no answer. He moves around the room aimlessly. He pauses by a wall, pokes it with his fist. Then he moves downstage again, almost up to the footlights. He punches his head lightly, self-admonishingly. He mutters*) Jerk. Jerk. What are you doing? Jerk.

(*He continues to move around the room.*)

Curtain

ACT TWO

ACT TWO

SCENE I

Three months have passed since the preceding act. The curtain rises on THE GIRL's *apartment. It is nighttime, about eight o'clock. There are lights in every room, even in the foyer. Some changes have been made in the apartment. There is now a day bed in* THE KID SISTER's *room, in addition to the bed that was there before.* THE GIRL *apparently shares the bedroom; it has the look of a room shared by two girls.*

In the living room THE KID SISTER *sits at the table, hunched over her textbooks. A middle-aged woman in a housecoat with a flowered pattern on it, whom we shall call* THE NEIGHBOR, *perches on the soft chair. A young woman in her late twenties, carrying a small parcel as well as her purse, is leaning against the doorjamb of the living-room doorway. We shall call her* THE FRIEND.

THE NEIGHBOR

Oh, the whole neighborhood has gone to pot. It's practically Harlem. The whole block is Puerto Rican.

> (THE MOTHER *appears, coming up the stairs. She wears a hat, a black winter coat with a fur collar, wet with snow, and carries a purse.*)

THE FRIEND

Well, I used to live on Ninety-eighth Street, just off the park, you know.

THE NEIGHBOR

Oh, sure. What the hell.

THE FRIEND

That used to be a very nice neighborhood.

THE NEIGHBOR

Oh, sure, absolutely.
(THE MOTHER *inserts her key into the lock. The sound of the door being opened attracts* THE FRIEND'S *attention. She looks casually down the foyer to the front door.*)

THE FRIEND

I live up in Washington Heights now with my husband, there's a lot of Puerto Ricans up there.

THE NEIGHBOR

Well, that's the way it is, sure.

THE FRIEND

(*To* THE MOTHER, *as she enters the apartment*)
Hello, Mrs. Mueller, how are you?

THE MOTHER

(*She can't quite make out who is greeting her from her position in the apartment doorway*)
Who's that?

52

THE KID SISTER

(*Looking up from her texts*)
Who's that, my mother?

THE FRIEND

(*To* THE MOTHER, *who is closing the front door now*)
This is Marilyn, Mrs. Mueller.

THE MOTHER

Hello, Marilyn, how are you, dear? Oh, it's really snowing out.
(THE KID SISTER *gets up, joins* THE FRIEND *at the living-room doorway, waiting for* THE MOTHER *to come up the foyer.*)

THE FRIEND

(*To* THE MOTHER)
I was downtown, so my husband took the kids over to his mother's, so I thought I'd just drop up, see if Betty wants to go to a movie.

THE KID SISTER

(*To* THE MOTHER, *now visible at the living-room doorway—conspiratorially*)
Ma, you better get dressed because he's coming over here. I came home, and Betty was just going in to take a shower—she's in the shower now—so she says, "Don't start walking around the house in your underwear, because Mr. Kingsley's coming over tonight."

53

THE MOTHER

What do you mean, Mr. Kingsley is coming over here tonight?

THE KID SISTER

I came home, Betty was getting undressed, and she told me. . . .

THE MOTHER

What time's he coming over?

THE KID SISTER

I don't know. She went in to take a shower, so then Mrs. Carroll rang the bell, so . . .

THE NEIGHBOR

Hello, Mrs. Mueller, how are you?

THE MOTHER

I'm fine, Mrs. Carroll, how are you?

THE KID SISTER

So I thought it was him.

THE NEIGHBOR

The whole neighborhood is turning Puerto Rican, I'll tell you that. I was just talking about that with this young lady here.

THE MOTHER

(*To* THE KID SISTER)

Where is she, in the shower?

THE KID SISTER

She went in about fifteen minutes ago.

THE MOTHER

(*To* THE FRIEND)

Do you know who we're talking about?

THE FRIEND

Yes, I know, because . . .

THE MOTHER

(*To* THE KID SISTER)

What did she say exactly? He's coming over tonight? She didn't tell me nothing about his coming over. Well, I'd like to get a look at him.

(*She has unbuttoned her coat, and we see now that she is wearing the white uniform of the bakery clerk.*)

THE FRIEND

Mrs. Mueller, I talked to Betty about this at length, and she is absolutely infatuated with this man, and my advice to you is just let the affair run its course.

THE MOTHER

Well, I'll tell you, I'm worried sick about it. I was thinking about it all day, and I had no appetite at all. (*She moves to a*

55

chair and sits down, addressing most of her comments to THE
NEIGHBOR) Because she sees him three and four times a week.
He's fifty-two, you know. She told me that just yesterday. I
had no idea he was that old. I thought he was in his late
thirties, and that was bad enough. Because I told her, you
know, "There's plenty of young fellows your own age." Because a man, fifty-two, what the hell does he want with a kid
like her except for you-know-what? Oh, God knows what she
does with him.

THE FRIEND

Mrs. Mueller, I wouldn't interfere with her.

THE MOTHER

Oh, my God, I live in a living terror she's going to come
in some night while I'm in bed and tell me she's pregnant.

THE FRIEND

She can take care of herself, Mrs. Mueller.

THE MOTHER

She's only a kid, for God's sakes. She ain't got much more
sense than Alice here. I always favored Alice. The living
truth is, I didn't want Betty when she was born. She came almost a month early. I had a terrible fight with my husband,
that's what brought her on. I didn't even want to see her after
she was born. That old Irish lady that was living next door
took care of her.
(*She stares, quite pained, at the others in the room.*)

THE FRIEND

Mrs. Mueller, a lot of girls find older men attractive because they're debonair and know a lot of tricks. I have a girl friend who went with a married man for eight years, and she finally had a nervous breakdown.

THE MOTHER

(*Not exactly heartened by this piece of news, turns to* THE NEIGHBOR)

When she was born, there was an Irish lady lived next door, gave her the formula and diapered her and everything. I didn't do a thing for a month.

THE NEIGHBOR

Oh, sure, what the hell.

THE MOTHER

(*Turns to her younger daughter, whose attention is far more with the talk than with her texts*)
You're not supposed to be listening to any of this.

THE FRIEND

I knew a girl in my neighborhood who was running around with a man in his forties. She had to have an abortion, but everything turned out all right.

THE MOTHER

(*Stands, mutters*)
You're full of cheerful anecdotes today, Marilyn.

THE FRIEND

Mrs. Mueller, I know Betty for six years now, and she's got a good head on her shoulders.

THE MOTHER

(*Taking off her coat, frowns*)
Well, I won't say nothing to her no more.

THE FRIEND

She's having a big romance right now. She thinks she's going out with Spencer Tracy. But in the bottom of her heart, she's still crazy about George.

THE MOTHER

(*Moving to the living-room door*)
Well, I won't interfere because she doesn't listen to anything I say anyway. She's always had her own way, and I gave up long ago trying to tell her anything. (*Apparently* THE GIRL *is coming out of the bathroom because* THE MOTHER *abruptly looks down the foyer toward the bathroom and cries out*) This is the last time you're going out with that man, do you hear me, Betty! (*To the others*) This is the last time she's going out with that man.

> (THE GIRL *now appears in the bedroom, closing the door behind her. She has obviously just finished taking a shower. She is wearing a pink peignoir and is vigorously toweling her hair. She reacts expressionlessly to her mother's outburst.* THE MOTHER *scowls and disappears off into her own room.*)

THE NEIGHBOR

Well, I suppose I ought to get up and go, but, to tell you the truth, I'd like to get a look at the fellow myself.

(*She exits off after* THE MOTHER. THE FRIEND, *standing in the foyer but still visible through the open doorway, now decides to go to* THE GIRL. *She turns and disappears behind the wall of the living room, knocks on the bedroom door, and* THE GIRL, *who is perched on the edge of her bed, toweling her hair, looks up.*)

THE GIRL

What?

THE FRIEND

(*Through the closed door*)
Can I come in a minute, Betty?

THE GIRL

Sure, come on in. (*The door opens and* THE FRIEND *comes in. She closes the door carefully behind her*) I didn't know you were here, Marilyn.

THE FRIEND

I yelled at you through the shower, but I guess you didn't hear me.

THE GIRL

How long you been here?

THE FRIEND

I just came in about fifteen minutes ago. I was downtown at Macy's, so I called Frank, and he said he was going to take the kids over to his mother's house, so, you know, I can't stand her, so I told him I'd probably go to a downtown movie here.

THE GIRL

Well, I got a date tonight.

THE FRIEND

Oh, I know. (THE FRIEND *sits down on* THE KID SISTER'S *bed. There is a short pause*) Well, how you feel?

THE GIRL

Fine.
  (*She stands, the towel draped over her head, goes to the chest of drawers, opens a drawer and searches around for something.*)

THE FRIEND

You hear anything from George?

THE GIRL

(*Fiddling around in the drawer*)
Oh, he called three times last week all the way from Las Vegas. Three o'clock in the morning he called once.

THE FRIEND

What did he have to say?
(THE GIRL *finally finds what she has been looking for—
several nylon stockings, which she holds up and ex-
amines for runs.*)

THE GIRL

(*After a moment*)
Well, I wrote him a letter about a week ago. I asked him for
a divorce. (*She has found two matching stockings with no
runs and returns to the bed and begins to put on her stockings.
After she has put the first one on, she pauses*) I finally went up
to see this lawyer last week. You remember Carol McKeever?
Her brother, he's a lawyer. So he told me the cheapest way
to get a divorce is to go to Mexico. So I said, "Oh, boy." So it
really isn't so complicated. It costs about seven hundred and
fifty dollars, the plane tickets and everything. So I wrote
George, and I asked him for a divorce, I sent the letter regis-
tered, airmail, special delivery. The next night, I swear to God,
George was on the phone from Las Vegas. So we must have
talked about twenty minutes. Oh, boy, I wonder what he paid
for that call. He called from his hotel room. He was calling
between shows. Frank Sinatra is out there now. So, anyway,
he called again about three o'clock in the morning after the
last show. Of course, it's only twelve o'clock out there, but he
should have realized there's a time difference. He woke up the
whole house. My mother got on the phone. She doesn't know
I wrote this letter to him. So I couldn't really talk to him with
my mother hanging all over me. So I told him to call me the
next day at six o'clock because my mother don't get home till
around seven-thirty. So he called me, and we had a long talk,

and he was all broken up. He was saying all kinds of wild things like he was going to take the next plane. So I told him, my mind was made up. So he finally said he wouldn't contest the divorce. So that's the last I heard from him. That was last Thursday. No, Friday.

(*She starts on the second stocking.*)

THE FRIEND

Are you really going to go through with this divorce?

THE GIRL

Don't tell my mother, because she doesn't know about it.
(*She stands now, back to the audience, and garters her stockings.*)

THE FRIEND

I'm your friend, Betty, and I'm going to tell you something right from the shoulder. You're making a big mistake.
(THE GIRL *rises again, goes to the open closet, fishes around in the incredibly crowded rack of clothes for a skirt, finds the one she wants.*)

THE GIRL

I know you feel that way, Marilyn.

THE FRIEND

What do you figure, to marry this man?

THE GIRL

If he asks me. I think I'm happy, Marilyn. I can't tell you how I feel in so many words, but life seems very pleasant to me right now. I even get along with my mother. I think I'm in love. Seriously in love. I feel so full sometimes it just wells up in me, my feelings for him. He went away for three days on a business trip to Detroit, I thought I'd die before he came back.

(*She has taken off her peignoir and is in her slip and stockinged feet. She quickly slips the skirt over her head and adjusts it.*)

THE FRIEND

Boy, he must be some operator, this guy.

(THE GIRL *frowns, regards her friend with some irritation.*)

THE GIRL

You want to know something? In the whole three months, he hasn't touched me once. I know what my mother thinks. She thinks I walk out of this door, I head straight for a hotel somewheres. Do you know where we go? We go dancing. We go driving. We go to a restaurant, we sit and talk for five hours. He hasn't put a hand on me in the whole three months.

THE FRIEND

Is that good?

THE GIRL

No, it isn't good. I think he's afraid of getting too involved with me.

(*She picks up a blouse that has been lying on the* KID
SISTER'S *bed.*)

THE FRIEND

What I mean is, do you think he's going to be able to satisfy
you sexually?

THE GIRL

(*Putting on her blouse. She is disturbed by the question*)
All I know is I can't wait to see him all the time.

THE FRIEND

Betty, you're jumping into a marriage, and you have to be a
little realistic too. In ten years he's going to be sixty-three and
you're going to be thirty-four. Do you think you're going to
be happy with a sixty-three-year-old husband in ten years?
Think about that a minute. A sixty-three-year-old husband
with white hair. You're a kid, you know that? You really are.
What do you think life is, a Street and Smith love story magazine? You had a good marriage with George. You paid the
rent and you went to bed. What are you looking for?

THE GIRL

Well, I'm looking for more than that.
(*She is quite disturbed now. She buttons her blouse,
stands before the mirror on the chest of drawers, surveys
herself.* THE FRIEND *scowls down at her feet.* THE GIRL
now begins to apply make-up. THE FRIEND *extracts a
pack of cigarettes from* THE GIRL'S *purse, lights one.*

THE MANUFACTURER *now appears, coming up the stairs to the landing. He wears his winter coat and his hat, both marked by what must be a fairly heavy snow outside. He stands before the door of the apartment but makes no move to ring the bell.)*

THE FRIEND

You want to know what life is? You live, that's all. That's life. You get married, you have kids—you get up in the morning and you go to sleep at night. Frank goes bowling every Thursday, and I manage to get down to Macy's once a week, and that's it, and it's not so bad. I don't know what you mean by happiness. You had a good marriage with George. At least he was hungry for you all the time. It was all over his face. That's more than most of us can say about our husbands.

THE GIRL

Are you having trouble with Frank, Marilyn?

THE FRIEND

Frank and me? We get along fine. We're perfectly happy. He stays out of my way and I stay out of his. You know, I envy you George, you know that? You have a husband who's crazy about you. Sure, he has his faults. He's a little selfish. He's a little conceited. But he doesn't go bowling on Thursday nights or stay up reading a magazine all night long. And one thing you know for sure, he isn't going to be sixty-three in ten years. You're going to want to have children, Betty. How do you know he's going to be able to give you kids? Because after a couple of years, that's all there really is, the kids.

(THE MANUFACTURER *has decided to ring the doorbell. It buzzes raucously, interrupting* THE FRIEND's *speech.* THE GIRL *looks up nervously. In the living room, the ringing of the doorbell has galvanized everybody into action.* THE NEIGHBOR *pops into the room, straightens out her housedress, and sits.* THE KID SISTER *stands at her table, not quite knowing what to do.* THE MOTHER *now appears in the living-room doorway, having changed into her black church dress.*)

THE MOTHER

(*Calling to* THE GIRL's *room*)

Betty, you going to answer the door?

THE GIRL

(*Calling back*)

I'll be right out.

THE FRIEND

(*To* THE GIRL)

You want me to answer the door?

THE GIRL

Please, Marilyn, would you? (*She is hurriedly applying her make-up. She looks anxiously at her friend*) Now don't expect anything special.

(THE FRIEND *opens the door and starts down the foyer.*)

THE KID SISTER

(*In the living room*)
Where should I go, should I stay here!

THE NEIGHBOR

(*In the living room, to* THE MOTHER)
I'll just stay back here out of the way.

THE FRIEND

(*Now passing* THE MOTHER, *who is still standing in the living-room doorway*)
I'll let him in, Mrs. Mueller. (*She reappears a moment later, coming down the foyer to the front door.* THE MOTHER *looks down the foyer, blatantly curious about* THE MANUFACTURER'S *appearance. In the bedroom,* THE GIRL *is not as in control of herself as she would like to be. She was considerably disturbed by the scene with her friend. She has to pause now in her hurried application of cosmetics to allow a deep sigh. She closes her eyes and tries to regain the composure she showed at first. In the foyer* THE FRIEND *opens the door to admit* THE MANUFACTURER) How do you do?

THE MANUFACTURER

How do you do? My name is Kingsley.

THE FRIEND

How do you do? I'm Betty's friend Marilyn. Won't you come in, please?

67

MIDDLE OF THE NIGHT

THE MANUFACTURER

Well, I'll tell you, I'm soaking wet with snow here, and I wouldn't want to dirty up your carpets.

(THE MOTHER *edges onto the landing.*)

THE MOTHER

How do you do there?

THE MANUFACTURER

How do you do?

THE MOTHER

Come in the house, for heaven's sakes.

THE MANUFACTURER

Well, I'll tell you, we're a little late as it is, and I have tickets here for a play, so just to come in for a couple of minutes, it really isn't worth the trouble.

THE MOTHER

Well, give me your coat, I'll hang it up in the bathroom.

THE MANUFACTURER

Thank you, I'm fine.

THE MOTHER

Well, I'm Betty's mother, how do you do?

THE MANUFACTURER

How do you do, Mrs. Mueller?

THE MOTHER

Would you excuse me a minute?

THE MANUFACTURER

Yes, certainly.

THE MOTHER

(*Going into the living room*)
He don't look like no Spencer Tracy to me. (*At the bedroom door, to* THE GIRL) He's waiting outside.

THE GIRL

(*From the bedroom*)
I'll be right out.
(THE MOTHER *goes back to the landing, followed by* THE KID SISTER *and* THE NEIGHBOR, *so that the landing suddenly seems embarrassingly crowded.*)

THE FRIEND

(*To* THE MANUFACTURER)
I happen to be here because my husband is taking the kids to my mother-in-law's and I don't happen to get along with her, so I thought I'd go to a downtown movie. It's really snowing out, isn't it?

THE MANUFACTURER

Yes, it's coming down quite heavily.

THE MOTHER

I told her you was here. This is my younger daughter, Alice. She's seventeen. She goes to George Washington High School. And this is my neighbor, Mrs. Carroll.

THE NEIGHBOR

(*Mumbling*)

Neighbor Mrs. Carroll . . .

THE MOTHER

She always comes in when I have dinner, to pass the time of day.

THE NEIGHBOR

(*Mumbling*)

Pass the time of day.

THE MANUFACTURER

Well, I'm very pleased to meet you all. (*An uncomfortable silence falls over the group*) Really, you don't have to stand here on my account. I'd come in, believe me, except I would leave pools of water everywhere.

(*Again the silence.*)

THE NEIGHBOR

We was just talking about the deterioration of the neighbor-hood. It's practically Harlem. There's nothing but colored people and Puerto Ricans living here now.

(*She seems to have said everything that needed to be said. Again the silence.*)

THE MOTHER

Well, Betty'll be right out.

(THE FRIEND *abruptly detaches herself from the group and disappears down the foyer in the direction of* THE GIRL'S *room.*)

THE MANUFACTURER

Well, the Puerto Ricans, after all, they have to have a place to live, too. In my business, which is the garment business, the operators are paid a thirty-two dollar a week minimum, and nowadays the young women don't care to work for such a salary. And, of course, we were faced with a serious competitive threat from the southern garment manufacturers. There's no unions down there, you understand. And frankly we have found that the Puerto Rican women are fine workers, very intelligent, very industrious. So that's the situation.

THE NEIGHBOR

(*After considering this address for a moment*)

He's absolutely right. The whole neighborhood's gone to pot.

(THE FRIEND *knocks on* THE GIRL'S *door and walks right in.* THE GIRL, *examining herself in front of the mirror, looks up quickly.*)

THE GIRL

(Nervously)
What do you think of him?

THE FRIEND

(Who really didn't think too much of him)
He seems very nice.

THE MOTHER

(On the landing, suddenly, to THE MANUFACTURER*)*
Would you like me to hang your coat in the shower?

THE MANUFACTURER

No, no, I'm fine.
*(*THE MOTHER *nods and goes quickly to the bedroom.)*

THE MOTHER

(Enters, more confused than anything else)
Is he a Jewish man, for God's sakes?
*(*THE GIRL *whirls on her mother, her composure completely shattered.)*

THE GIRL

(Crying out)
So what?!

THE MOTHER

Well, I just asked, that's all.

72

THE FRIEND

(*To* THE MOTHER)

Maybe we better get out and leave Betty finish up.

THE GIRL

(*Looking in the closet for a coat*)

I'm all finished.

THE MOTHER

(*To* THE GIRL)

Where are you going tonight?

(THE GIRL *rips her coat off the hanger and faces her mother furiously.*)

THE GIRL

We're not going to a hotel, if that's what you want to know! In the whole three months, he hasn't put a hand on me! Is that what you want to know?

THE MOTHER

All right, all right, he can hear every word you're saying.

(THE GIRL *pulls the door open and strides out into the foyer. A moment later, she is on the landing.*)

THE GIRL

(*To* THE MANUFACTURER)

All right, I'm ready, Jerry, let's go.

(THE MANUFACTURER *nods, turns to* THE NEIGHBOR *and* THE KID SISTER.)

THE MANUFACTURER

Well, good-bye, it was nice to have met you.

THE NEIGHBOR

Good-bye, sir.

(THE KID SISTER *nods.* THE MANUFACTURER *looks quickly at* THE GIRL.)

THE MANUFACTURER

(*To* THE MOTHER, *who is now on the landing*)
Well, good-bye, Mrs. Mueller.

THE MOTHER

Good-bye, Mr. Kingsley.

THE FRIEND

Good-bye, Mr. Kingsley.

(THE MANUFACTURER *looks at* THE GIRL, *who is slipping into her coat. She is obviously disturbed. The others all go into the living room.*)

THE MOTHER

(*In a heavy whisper, to* THE NEIGHBOR)
He's a Jewish man, you know.

THE NEIGHBOR

Oh, sure, what the hell.

(*On the landing,* THE MANUFACTURER *has started for the stairs, but pauses when he sees* THE GIRL *is making no move to follow him.*)

MIDDLE OF THE NIGHT

THE MANUFACTURER

Is something wrong, Betty?

THE GIRL

(*Turns to* THE MANUFACTURER, *keeping her eyes down*)
I want to go somewheres with you tonight, you know what
I mean? (THE MANUFACTURER *looks at her, not quite knowing what she means*) I want to go to a hotel. I think it's
time we went to a hotel.

THE MANUFACTURER

(*After a moment*)
We can go to my house. I don't want to go to a hotel.
(THE MANUFACTURER *turns and starts down the stairs.
She follows him. They both disappear from view.*)

THE MOTHER

(*In the living room*)
I never was much of a mother to her. She keeps throwing
that up to me. I want to do the right thing this time. You
know what I mean?

THE NEIGHBOR

Oh, sure, what the hell.

The lights fade slowly

Scene 2

THE MANUFACTURER'S *apartment, later that night. The only light on is the dim one in the anteroom, which casts just enough light for us to see into the darkened living room. After a moment,* THE GIRL *appears in the anteroom, entering from another part of the apartment. She is wearing the dress she wore in the preceding scene, but is adjusting it as though she has just put it on. She is in her stockinged feet. The light in the anteroom is so inadequate that we can barely make out more than her silhouette. Her hair is disheveled, and she begins to straighten it. As she does, she steps down into the living room, finds a lamp and turns it on. A soft cone of light spreads across much of the room. We can see now that her coat and* THE MANUFACTURER'S *have been dropped on the davenport and on a chair, that her purse is on the floor, and that her shoes lie tumbled on their sides in the middle of the room.*

She moves to her shoes, straightens them with her toes, and squeezes her feet into them. Throughout all this, she has been soddenly expressionless. Now she closes her eyes and just stands, letting a sigh escape. Then she shakes her head and picks up her purse and puts it on the end table.

THE MANUFACTURER *now appears in the anteroom. He is in his shirt sleeves and does not wear a tie. He stands in the anteroom, watching* THE GIRL, *who is aware of his presence but does not turn to him.*

The entire scene is shadowed and silhouetted.

76

THE MANUFACTURER

(*Gently*)

Would you like something, a cup of coffee or anything like that? (THE GIRL *shakes her head, does not turn to him.* THE MANUFACTURER *moves down into the living room, to the window, touches the radiator cover under the window*) One thing I can say about this building, there's always steam. This is something from my childhood. I don't care what I have to pay rent as long as I got steam in the winter. (THE GIRL *opens her purse, takes out her lipstick, sits on the davenport and begins to apply it.* THE MANUFACTURER *regards her with a slight, almost hurt smile*) It wasn't such a good idea, after all.

THE GIRL

(*Looks briefly up and then back to her lipstick*)

Oh, I'm all right.

(THE MANUFACTURER *turns away, apparently disturbed.* THE GIRL *pauses in the application of her lipstick, lets her hands fall to her lap.* THE MANUFACTURER *looks back at her, almost angrily.*)

THE MANUFACTURER

Please, Betty, don't put on lipstick. To jump out of bed and put on lipstick, it's like a whore. (*He turns away again, edgy, angry with himself for being irritable.* THE GIRL *sits miserably, her hands in her lap.* THE MANUFACTURER *sits down several chairs away from her*) Listen, did you know Lockman tried to commit suicide yesterday?

THE GIRL

(*Looks up, startled*)

Mr. Lockman?

THE MANUFACTURER

He called his wife from a hotel, and he said he was going to take fifty sleeping pills. So she called me, so I called the police. That's what all the fuss in the office was about yesterday. That's why I had to run out. We broke down the door, and they took him to Bellevue. Oh, my God, what a time that was. (*He stands again, shaken a little*) I know what you think about Walter Lockman. He's always pinching you and flirting. He wasn't that way till the last couple of years. He's a kind, generous man. (*He turns to* THE GIRL, *almost pleading*) I told the psychiatrist there, I said, "This man, my partner, whom I know for twenty-odd years," I told the psychiatrist, I said, "He's getting old, and he's so terrified of being impotent." That's why he flirts so much. That's why he runs around with buyers and prostitutes from hotels. You have to understand the torture and the doubts that a man has when he reaches middle age.

THE GIRL

I'm not angry with him, Jerry.

(THE MANUFACTURER *straightens up, walks away a few paces. He sits down, his mind heavy with his thoughts. He looks across to* THE GIRL.)

THE MANUFACTURER

There was a hundred times in the last couple of months when it would have been better than tonight. At least a hundred times, where I looked at you and I had tears in my eyes, I had such a gentleness for you. Love is a gentle business, Betty. Because this way, this way . . . I'll tell you what it was like this way. About five, six months ago, Walter Lockman came to me, he says, "Listen, I'm taking out a buyer tonight. We'll go to the Copa. We'll go to the Bon Soir down in the Village. We'll get a couple of girls. Come on. We'll have a good time." This is the wheels of industry operating. Some of these buyers come in, you don't get them a girl, they won't order fifty dozen blouses. All right, so I was lonely, so I said all right. (*He stands, angry with the memory of the incident. He moves around as he tells the story*) So I came home and took a shave. I put on a new suit. I went with them down the Bon Soir. They had three girls. Nice-looking girls. You be surprised how nice-looking some of these girls are. So I got a little drunk there. I made a lot of jokes. Listen, sometimes, I can be pretty witty. Everybody was laughing. We got in a cab, and we went to a hotel on Thirty-second Street. Lockman had a suite of rooms there. Oh, I'm telling you. We were laughing in the cab, and we were laughing in the elevator. Everything I said, my girl would fall over from laughter. So we got in the room, this girl with me keeps pulling me by the arm into the bedroom.

THE GIRL

(*Mumbling*)
I don't want to hear about it, Jerry.

THE MANUFACTURER

So let me tell you. So we got in the bedroom, and my girl kept hanging all over me. So we closed the door, so she turned to me, she said, "You'll have to pay the fifty dollars first." At the risk of being a little dramatic, I was sick. (*He sits down again on still another chair*) I thought she liked me, you know what I mean? (*With his hand he kneads his brow nervously and absently*) Well, to make a long story short, as soon as it was over, she got right up, she began putting on lipstick.

THE GIRL

(*With deep tenderness*)

I love you, Jerry, from the bottom of my heart.

(*For a brief moment, they regard each other with a strange, delicate pain.*)

THE MANUFACTURER

(*Turning away, feeling tears*)

I wasn't pleading for Lockman before, sweetheart. I was pleading for myself.

THE GIRL

I know. I want to marry you, Jerry.

THE MANUFACTURER

I'm afraid to. I'm afraid. I knew tonight was going to happen sooner or later. I kept pushing it off. I didn't want to touch what we had. It meant so much to me. I had a new life with you. I didn't want to think about marriage. I'm afraid of such a marriage. I'm afraid of myself. At my age, you become afraid of things. You begin to be conscious of your fingers, that they're not as clever as they used to be. Your legs get tired from standing fifteen minutes. Your whole body resists you. I don't know what I'll be like in five years, Betty. I don't want a five-year marriage.

(*He turns away again, shielding his eyes, the tears flooding up in him again.*)

THE GIRL

Let's not make problems. I'm not worried about what's going to happen in five years.

THE MANUFACTURER

(*Sits*)

I told my sister today I've been seeing a lot of you.

THE GIRL

What did she say?

THE MANUFACTURER

Well, she suspected, of course, that I was seeing somebody, but she was a little upset when I told her it was you and how young you were.

THE GIRL

I'm the big scandal of my family. All my aunts and uncles and my cousin Loretta were over the house the other night, and she called you my sugar daddy. And my mother picked it up, and that's all I've been hearing the last couple of days, all about my sugar daddy. (*He says nothing; he is still troubled by deep, anxious thoughts. She senses this*)

Don't break up with me, Jerry.

(*For a moment,* THE MANUFACTURER *looks at her, somewhat distracted.*)

81

THE MANUFACTURER

You know what I did tonight?

THE GIRL

What?

THE MANUFACTURER

I came out of the office, I was going to take a cab to go to the garage to get the car. So it was just starting to snow and the air was so clear. So you know what I did?

THE GIRL

What?

THE MANUFACTURER

I walked all the way up from the office to the garage.

THE GIRL

Oh, for Pete's sake.

THE MANUFACTURER

That's forty blocks. That's a good two miles.

THE GIRL

That's wonderful. (*Pause*) Please ask me to marry you, Jerry.

THE MANUFACTURER

I'll tell you what honest to God bothers me. I love you, Betty. My whole life has been a pleasure since I know you.

82

A pleasure to wake up, a pleasure to go to work. I cherish you. I cherish you like you were a diamond, but I'm afraid in a couple of years I'll be like Lockman. I'll be running around with prostitutes. It won't matter any more if they like me.

THE GIRL

Jerry . . .

THE MANUFACTURER

Pay them the fifty dollars already!

THE GIRL

I don't know what to do when you're this way.

THE MANUFACTURER

(*Mounting panic*)
I'll tell you what I'm really afraid of. I'm afraid in a couple of years you'll start looking around for a younger man!

THE GIRL

I would never do that.

THE MANUFACTURER

What do you see in me, Betty? I'm like a father to you!

THE GIRL

No!

THE MANUFACTURER

You never had a father. I'm like a father to you!

83

THE GIRL

It's more than that! You know that! I'll make you happy. I promise you I'll make you happy. What do you want me to do?

(*He turns away from her, and the two of them sit, afraid to look at each other.*)

THE MANUFACTURER

(*Muttering*)

If any of my friends told me he was going to marry a young girl, I would say, "Don't be a fool. It's not a healthy relationship."

(THE GIRL *looks at him now, her eyes wide and wet with tears.*)

THE GIRL

I love you, Jerry. I love you from the bottom of my heart.

(*They regard each other in a sudden stillness.*)

THE MANUFACTURER

Will you marry me, Betty? (*She moves to him, and they suddenly clutch at each other, embracing with an abrupt, fierce desperation. After a long moment, they release each other, and* THE MANUFACTURER *stands, deeply stirred. He shuffles a few paces away.* THE GIRL *stands, and he turns to look at her, and then he goes to her again, and they cling to each other, both crying quietly now in each other's arms*) Oh, my sweet girl, I love you so much, you don't know. (*They release each other again, and then* THE MANUFACTURER *sits down in one of the chairs, strangely exhilarated, yet confused and not quite understanding his own immense emotions. He seems a little abstracted. He looks up at* THE GIRL, *who stands, profoundly moved. Quietly*) If you change your mind to-morrow, I won't be angry with you. I want you to think about everything. I won't lie to you, Betty. I'm afraid.

(THE GIRL *nods absently. Then goes to the davenport and sits down again. They each sit now, quietly, touched a little with terror at the decisive step they have just taken.*)

The lights fade slowly

SCENE 3

The same night, later. THE MANUFACTURER'S *living room. One of the lamps is on, and there is another light on somewhere deeper in the apartment. No one is on stage at the moment.*

The front door opens and THE SISTER, THE DAUGHTER *and* THE SON-IN-LAW *enter. They are wearing winter coats.* THE SON-IN-LAW *is a tall, lean fellow in his early thirties. He wears a hat. He is an amiable, good-natured nebbisch sort of fellow.* THE SISTER *seems disturbed about something.*

THE SISTER

(*Turning on the anteroom light*)
There's a light on. I told you there was a light on. His jacket's on the chair there.

(THE DAUGHTER *moves into the living room, unbuttoning her coat, and, with a small sigh, sinks down into a chair. Her husband follows her a few steps.*)

THE DAUGHTER

(*To her husband*)

Maybe you better call home, tell the baby sitter we'll be a little late.

THE SON-IN-LAW

(*Moving to the phone*)

We going to be here that long?

(THE DAUGHTER *frowns.* THE SON-IN-LAW *dials.*)

THE SISTER

(*Peering nervously down into the apartment*)

Jerry, are you in the bathroom? I think there's a light on in the bathroom. Sit down a minute. I'll bring you some fruit.

(*She disappears into the apartment.*)

THE SON-IN-LAW

(*On phone*)

Hello, Bernice? This is Mr. Englander. How's the baby?
. . .

(THE SISTER *comes back into the anteroom, taking off her coat.*)

THE SISTER

(*Heading for the hall closet*)

He's in the bathroom. He'll be right out. I told him you was here.

THE DAUGHTER

(*To her aunt*)

I don't know what you want us to say to him, Evelyn.

THE SISTER

(*Hanging her coat in the closet*)

Don't say nothing. I wasn't supposed to tell you about this girl.

THE SON-IN-LAW

(*On phone*)

Listen, Bernice dear, we're going to be a little late, about one or one-thirty . . . (*He looks at his wife for confirmation, and she nods*) Sure, call your mother. I'll drive you home, so don't worry . . .

(THE SISTER *moves into the living room now, a little distraught, her hands twisting restlessly.*)

THE SISTER

We're sitting down to dinner, he says to me, "I've been going out with a girl." So I thought a forty-five-year-old girl, a fifty-year-old girl. It comes out later it's a twenty-four-year-old girl. I couldn't eat. I didn't say nothing. I kept my mouth shut. But I was sick.

(*She sits down, her fingers moving restlessly on the arms of the chair. She sighs nervously.*)

THE DAUGHTER

Evelyn, why are you so worked up? My father is having a middle-aged fling.

THE SISTER

It's not a fling. If it was a fling, would he tell me? Your father doesn't make flings.

THE DAUGHTER

Do you feel he intends to marry the girl?

THE SISTER

I don't know. (*Stands suddenly*) I forgot the fruit.
(*She starts off for the kitchen again.*)

THE DAUGHTER

What exactly did he say to you, Evelyn?

THE SISTER

Look, he's coming out in a minute, so let's drop the subject. I didn't tell you nothing. You don't know nothing about it.

THE DAUGHTER

We don't know nothing.
(THE SISTER *disappears into the apartment.* THE DAUGHTER *stares at her shoes with a vague scowl.* THE SON-IN-LAW *finds a chair, sits down, his opened coat falling to his sides.*)

THE SON-IN-LAW

(*After a moment*)

So what do you say, Lillian, about Monday? (*His wife looks up at him, not quite knowing what he's talking about*)

We always wind up my vacations sitting in the backyard. I was talking to Paul there, as I was telling you, before Evelyn started this whole business, and he said, and Elizabeth said, they'd take the kid off our hands for the two weeks. What the hell, we took their Richard when they went to the Poconos last summer.

THE DAUGHTER

Do you remember any blonde up in my father's office, Jack?

THE SON-IN-LAW

I haven't been up there in a couple of years.

THE DAUGHTER

Oh, wait a minute. Yes, I do. There's a blonde up there. Sits in front of Caroline. A very sweet-looking girl.
(*She frowns slightly.*)

THE SON-IN-LAW

So, what'll I tell my boss? Shall I tell him I'll take the vacation Monday? I'll tell you, Lillian. I'd like to get away. I'm tired, and the snow and the slush. The tax season starts in a couple of weeks, and I'll be working nights. I'd like to get away, I think.

THE DAUGHTER

(*Not really interested*)
Elizabeth said she'd take the baby?

THE SON-IN-LAW

Sure. We took their Richard when they went to the Poconos. (*He stands, feeling in his coat pockets for cigarettes. He sends a brief look over to his wife, who is sitting, apparently concerned with her own thoughts*) I don't know. It seems to me it wouldn't hurt us to get away somewheres and relax. I feel there's a tenseness between us. I don't know. It seems that . . . I don't know . . .

(*He lights his cigarette, wishing he hadn't brought up the matter.*)

THE DAUGHTER

What do you mean, tenseness?

THE SON-IN-LAW

I don't know. It seems we never talk or go out. It seems . . .

THE DAUGHTER

We went out tonight.

THE SON-IN-LAW

I don't know what I mean. I come home, and we have dinner, and you tell me about the baby, or your father comes over, or . . .

THE DAUGHTER

My father hasn't been up the house in three weeks.

THE SON-IN-LAW

Listen, I like your father. I wasn't objecting to his coming over.

THE DAUGHTER

I don't know what you mean by tenseness.

THE SON-IN-LAW

Well, maybe that's the wrong word, I just feel that . . .

THE DAUGHTER

We've been married more than three years, Jack.

THE SON-IN-LAW

No! No! It's not that. Listen, I like your father. He's a
prince of a man.
  (THE DAUGHTER *crosses to the end table, on which her
  purse lies.*)

THE DAUGHTER

(*Fishing in her purse, apparently for her cigarettes. She
smiles*)
She's so funny, Evelyn. She's so upset about this girl.

THE SON-IN-LAW

(*Proffering his pack of cigarettes*)
Have one of mine, Lillian.

THE DAUGHTER

(*Shakes her head, gets one of her own out,
continues to smile*)
She was in a state when we went in to get our coats. She
comes over to me, she says, "I got something terrible to tell
you." I thought she was going to tell me she had cancer. So
she says, "Your father is seeing a girl, twenty-four years old."

91

So I looked at her, I said, "So?" (*She sits down, leans across to her husband*) You know what it is with her, Jack? Subconsciously, she thinks of herself as my father's wife. She resents any woman who gets close to him. She never got along with my mother. I didn't get along with my mother either, but that was an entirely different matter. So now she lives here in the house with him, and . . . I was against it, you know. When my mother died, and my father told me that Evelyn wanted to move in with him, I said, "Pop, you're just feeding her neurotic attachment for you." I wanted him to move in with us.

THE SON-IN-LAW

Listen, I was perfectly willing.

THE DAUGHTER

She resents me a great deal. Every time my father and I sit down for one of our little talks, she always finds some way of breaking in. She resents any woman my father likes. It's frankly a little incest, that's what it is.

(THE SON-IN-LAW *gestures with his head to remind her of* THE SISTER's *off-stage presence. They lower their voices.*)

THE SON-IN-LAW

Well, she's a lonely old woman, and . . .

THE DAUGHTER

So my father is going to bed with some girl, what's so terrible about it? (*She stands, moves nervously a few paces, puffs on her cigarette. She turns back to her husband*) I can see how a girl could go for my father. He's a damned attractive man. For a man with no formal education, he is amazingly literate. I wonder if he actually goes to bed with this little tramp.

THE SON-IN-LAW

Well, I assume . . .

THE DAUGHTER

He's got a lot of charm, my old man. (*She sits down again, smoking.* THE SON-IN-LAW *interests himself in the needlework of the doily on his chair.* THE DAUGHTER *leans toward him, lowers her voice, smiles, shakes her head*) What surprises me is my father didn't mention a word about this little affair of his to me. He usually tells me everything.

THE SON-IN-LAW

(*Smiles tentatively*)
Well, it's hardly something a father would tell his daughter.

THE DAUGHTER

It so happens we're pretty damn close, Jack. I'm probably closer to my father than to any other person I know.
(*Her husband looks quickly down, and* THE DAUGHTER *aware that this was something of a slight to her husband, flushes.*)

THE SON-IN-LAW

Listen, he's a prince of a man, your father. I'm the first one to admit it.
(THE DAUGHTER *stands, looks around for an ash tray, sees one across the room, crosses to it. A moment of silence.*)

THE DAUGHTER

What I meant was, in many ways, he's a remarkable man, and I respect him very much. (*She looks at her husband for a moment*) Jack, we'll go to Florida, Monday. I could do with a vacation myself, and you've been looking very tired recently.

THE SON-IN-LAW

Listen, why take the train down, and waste a whole day? We'll fly.

THE DAUGHTER

Elizabeth said she'd take the baby?

THE SON-IN-LAW

We got a couple of hotels down there for accounts, and I can get a room or a suite if you like, cheap.

THE DAUGHTER

I'll call Elizabeth tomorrow, see just how serious she is. Otherwise, we could leave the baby with your mother.

(*She breaks off as* THE SISTER *returns with a tray, on which there is a bowl of fruit.*)

THE SISTER

(*As she comes down into the room*)

You see, why should he tell me about it? I don't know what he does with his nights. I don't want to know. He calls up, he says he's not coming home for dinner. All right. That's his business. So why should he bother to tell me about this girl if it wasn't a serious business? I don't want him to do something he'll regret the rest of his life.

(THE DAUGHTER *whirls on* THE SISTER *as she sets the tray down on an end table.*)

THE DAUGHTER

(*Angrily*)

Evelyn! Leave him alone, you hear me! He's having a little fun for himself! Don't destroy it for him!

THE SISTER

(*Looking up, a little startled*)

What's the matter with you?

THE DAUGHTER

You're jealous of this girl! Any woman that gets close to my father, I resent . . . I mean you resent! He's having an affair! What are you so upset about?

THE SISTER

You seem more upset than me.

(THE DAUGHTER *turns angrily away, sits heavily down on a chair.*)

THE DAUGHTER

I don't want any fruit!

(THE SISTER *looks at* THE SON-IN-LAW.)

THE SISTER

What's the matter with her? I just don't want my brother to do something he'll regret the rest of his life.

(THE MANUFACTURER *suddenly calls out from deeper in the apartment.*)

THE MANUFACTURER

(*Off*)

Hello! I'll be right there!

THE SISTER

(*Calling back*)

All right, we got fruit. (*To* THE SON-IN-LAW) What did I say? I don't even know what I said that she suddenly starts yelling at me like that.

(THE MANUFACTURER *appears now, coming into the anteroom. He is in his shirt sleeves but wears a tie. He seems to be in excellent and hearty spirits.*)

THE MANUFACTURER

Hello, Jack boy, how are you there?

THE SON-IN-LAW

Hello, Jerry, how are you?

THE MANUFACTURER

(*Coming down into the living room*)

I just got in about half an hour ago myself. I was soaking wet. I was walking in the snow there. I took a hot shower, and I feel wonderful. Hello, Lillian sweetheart, how are you? Where were you all tonight, at Paul's? (*He has started for the fruit bowl but he is intercepted by his daughter, who stops him to give him a sudden embrace. He regards her with mild surprise*) Why such a big hug?

THE DAUGHTER

(*Still holding him*)

I haven't seen you in a couple of weeks, I missed you. I called every night last week, you wasn't in. What have you been doing with yourself?

THE MANUFACTURER

(*Releasing himself*)

Well, listen, give me some fruit, I'll tell you all about it.

THE SON-IN-LAW

We're going down to Florida Monday, Jerry, Lillian and me.

THE MANUFACTURER

(*Taking an apple*)

Hey, you lucky bums, you. But I'll tell you something. I like snow. All of a sudden, I like snow. I used to hate it. Remember, Lillian, how I used to hate the winter? Always I took my vacation in the winter. My wife and I, every winter. Florida, California. But now I go for walks. If I told you how much I walked in the snow tonight, and that's a blizzard out there. I'll bet you at least six, seven inches. I walked from the office to the garage. Forty-two blocks. It was so clear out. Like a lunatic, I started walking up Broadway. I got to a Hundred and Eighteenth Street, I suddenly stopped, I said, "What am I, crazy?" It was so bracing outside. I want you to know, Evelyn, I did not wear rubbers, I did not wear galoshes. I came home, I was soaking wet, and I feel wonderful. So you're going to Florida? Your first time, right? You'll have a wonderful time. It's the height of the season, Jack, did you make reservations? Evelyn, give me a knife. So when are you going,

97

Monday? Are you going by plane, train, what? (*He suddenly pauses while paring the apple and slaps the back of an upholstered chair*) I'm going to tell you something. I just feel wonderful. Listen, as long as you're here. I've got something to tell you. I figured I'd drive up tomorrow night and see you, but as long as you're here. I'll go see Paul tomorrow. How is he, by the way, and Elizabeth? I haven't seen them in a couple of weeks. Well, anyway, did Evelyn tell you anything?

THE SISTER

I didn't say nothing. You told me to say nothing, and that's what I said.

THE MANUFACTURER

Well, I've decided to get married again.
(THE DAUGHTER *goes for her cigarettes again.*)

THE DAUGHTER

You're going to get married, Pa?

THE MANUFACTURER

Well, I'll tell you the whole story.

THE DAUGHTER

(*Fishing in her purse for cigarettes*)
Do we know the woman, Pa?

THE MANUFACTURER

Well, you might. I don't know. She's a girl works up in my

98

office. You probably saw her there. A blond girl. The receptionist, sits in front of Caroline.

(THE SON-IN-LAW *again proffers his pack of cigarettes to his wife, who shakes her head and gets out one of her own.*)

THE SON-IN-LAW

Congratulations, Jerry.

THE MANUFACTURER

Thank you. I think you should know, she's quite a young girl. Twenty-four years old. She's younger than you are, Lillian. I've been seeing her for a couple of months, and it just seems that this is it.

(*The brief enthusiasm of the previous moment seems to have filtered out. A short silence fills the room.* THE SISTER, *who had turned abruptly away at* THE MANUFACTURER's *announcement, rubs her brow nervously with the tips of her fingers.* THE SON-IN-LAW *sends a cautious look to his wife and then looks back to the floor.* THE DAUGHTER *sits down again, takes a long puff on her cigarette.* THE MANUFACTURER *purses his lips.*)

THE DAUGHTER

(*Smiling briefly*)
Well, that's wonderful, Pa. I'm very happy for you.

THE MANUFACTURER

Thank you, sweetheart, thank you. Nothing definite has been set. The girl has to get a divorce, she's in the process now. I'd like you to meet the girl. I'm sure you'll like her. We'll have to set up some kind of dinner. (*He considers the carpet-*

ing at his feet, takes a deep sigh) So that's it, that's my announcement.

THE SISTER

(*Suddenly moves to her brother, bursting out*)
Jerry, what are you doing? Do you know what you're doing?
What's the matter with you?

THE MANUFACTURER

Evelyn, let me stop you before you even start.

THE SISTER

Honest to God, for God's sakes. All right, you come in, you
tell me, a twenty-four-year-old girl. All right. What's the matter with you? You're a sensible man, for the love of God,
honest to God. Our brother Herman, who is a fool—all right,
this I could expect from him. But you're the sensible one. For
God's sakes, what's the matter with you?
(THE MANUFACTURER *has moved a few steps toward his
daughter.*)

THE MANUFACTURER

(*To his daughter, with a vague smile*)
I have to admit, Lillian, I expected a little more enthusiasm
from you.
(THE DAUGHTER *looks up, smiles briefly.*)

THE DAUGHTER

I'm just a little shocked, Pa, to tell you the truth.

THE MANUFACTURER

It's really not such a shocking thing. I'm going to get married, that's all. Of course, she's a young girl, and this presents a number of problems, but . . .

THE SISTER

(*To* THE SON-IN-LAW)

It never works out. I could tell you ten cases. When I had my apartment in Brooklyn, there was a man in the building, fifty-nine years old, he ran away with a sixteen-year-old girl. It was in the papers and everything. What a scandal. His wife had a nervous breakdown. (*Turns to her brother*) Jerry, don't do something you'll regret the rest of your life. You're fifty-three years old. You're a man settled in habit. You like to come home, you watch television. You want to get married, marry somebody your own age. Who is this girl? I want to know. Who is this girl? She sees a nice rich fellow, has a good business, makes a good living. She sees herself living in a fancy apartment, fancy clothes. . . .

THE MANUFACTURER

Evelyn, don't get so excited. You're beginning to say a lot of foolish things.

THE SISTER

Is she going to move in here?

THE MANUFACTURER

A married couple usually live together.

THE SISTER

(*Throwing up her hands and moving away*)

All right! You want to marry her, marry her. You want me to move out of the house? All right, I'll pack my clothes, I'll move out.

THE MANUFACTURER

Is that what's bothering you?

THE SISTER

What's bothering me is you're making a fool of yourself.

THE DAUGHTER

All right, Evelyn . . .

THE SISTER

You're making a fool of yourself, Jerry. I'm telling you right to your face. All right, you want to have an affair with a girl, all right. But marriage? Don't be a fool. It never works out. Max Coleman—you remember Max Coleman? I could tell you a hundred cases. Max Coleman married a girl of thirty-four, already a young woman, not a kid any more, and you saw what happened. One year, and they were divorced. (THE MANUFACTURER *turns from his sister and moves slowly to his daughter.* THE SISTER *suddenly calls out*) Is she Jewish?

THE MANUFACTURER

(*Sitting down beside his daughter*)

Does that matter in this day and age?

THE SISTER

(*Paces nervously to another corner of the room, mutters*)
All right, you want me to move out, I'll pack my clothes, I'll move out.

(THE MANUFACTURER *looks at his daughter.*)

THE MANUFACTURER

Lillian, I sense you're not entirely happy about the whole idea.

THE DAUGHTER

Pa, for heaven's sakes, you come in the room, you tell me you're going to get married to some girl. Give me a chance to digest it.

THE SISTER

(*Calling out from her corner*)
Do you remember Harry Wolfson? Used to live on Eastern Parkway when we used to live in Brooklyn. He also had a big romance with a young girl. A man gets to middle age, and he begins to worry about . . .

THE MANUFACTURER

What's so terrible about middle age? I'm physically in tip-top shape. Nat Phillips has been trying to get me interested in golf. Son of a gun, I'm going to take him up on it.

THE SISTER

Max Coleman married a girl of thirty-four, already a young woman, not a kid any more, and in one year . . .

THE MANUFACTURER

Max Coleman is an idiot, was an idiot, and always will be.

THE SISTER

Jerry, we went to Paul's New Year's Eve party last year. A bunch of young people, dancing and drinking. Didn't you tell me you felt out of place? For heaven's sakes, your own daughter Lillian is older than this girl. A young girl, twenty years old, what does she want? She wants night clubs, dancing. She's not going to sit with you, watch television every night. And don't say you're in such tiptop shape. You're not such an athlete any more. You've been complaining about your back for a good couple of years.

THE MANUFACTURER

Don't you think I considered all this? I'm a businessman, you know. I don't jump into propositions.

THE SISTER

Are you kidding yourself this girl's in love with you or something?

THE MANUFACTURER

Evelyn, this is really none of your goddam business.

THE SISTER

You said you wanted to discuss it.

MIDDLE OF THE NIGHT

THE MANUFACTURER

(*With sudden sharpness*)

I made an announcement! I didn't open the floor for discussions! I'm not a kid we're deciding to send to summer camp or not. I'm not a family problem.

THE SISTER

(*Throwing up her hands and turning away*)

All right! All right!

THE DAUGHTER

All right, Pa . . .

THE SISTER

You want me to pack my clothes, I'll move out, that's all.

THE DAUGHTER

(*Taking the older woman's arm*)

All right, Evelyn, don't get so upset.

(THE SISTER's *eyes have become red.*)

THE SISTER

(*Shielding her eyes with a hand*)

My whole life I gave up for my brothers and sisters. My whole life. Mama died, who brought up the family? My whole life I gave up.

(*She turns away from the others, moves quickly across the room.*)

THE MANUFACTURER

Nobody said you have to move out. Maybe we'll get a bigger apartment. I don't know. I haven't thought about it.

THE SISTER

(*Shrilly*)

I wouldn't live in the same house with that tramp!

THE MANUFACTURER

(*Angrily*)

All right! Shut up!

THE DAUGHTER

All right, Pa, all right.

THE MANUFACTURER

For God's sakes, the world isn't coming to an end. I'm just going to get married.

THE DAUGHTER

(*Escorting him to a chair*)

All right, Pa, don't get so angry.

(*A sudden, swift, inexplicable silence sweeps over the room, thick with the edges of unresolved angers.* THE MANUFACTURER *plucks at his trouser leg with nervous fingers.* THE DAUGHTER *sits down on the couch. Then, suddenly,* THE SISTER *whirls abruptly and goes sullenly up into the anteroom, disappearing into the apartment.* THE MANUFACTURER *looks up briefly, scowling at her departing back. He mutters to no one in particular, but really to his daughter.*)

THE MANUFACTURER

All she's worried about is she's going to have to move out of the house. She's the older sister, you know, so she feels everybody has to get her okay. That's why Herman never got married, do you know that? She wouldn't approve of any girl.

THE DAUGHTER

Pa, her position in your house is threatened, and she's fighting, that's all.

THE MANUFACTURER

(*The anger flowing out of him*)

This was not an easy decision for me. To get married, you know, at my age, and to a girl young enough to be my daughter . . . Don't you think I have doubts about what I'm doing? You know Walter Lockman tried to commit suicide yesterday?

THE DAUGHTER

No, I didn't know, Pa.

THE MANUFACTURER

Everybody gets to a certain age there, when suddenly old age with white hair, sitting in the park playing checkers . . . who wants to be an old fool? I'll tell you something. It's important to me that a young girl finds me attractive. I didn't know it was so important, but it's important. (*He leans to his daughter, a vague note of pleading slipping into his voice*) She needs me, you understand, Lillian? It's been a long time since somebody needed me. My kids are all grown up, with children of their own. I'm a man who has to give of himself, I . . . (*He turns his face away and scowls. For a moment, nobody says anything. Then he stands, ostensibly looks for his jacket, which is draped over the back of the chair. He goes to it*) I don't have to justify myself. I decided to get married, that's all.

THE DAUGHTER

Nobody said no, Pa.

THE MANUFACTURER

(*Finding a cigar and taking it out*)
She's a very sweet girl. Very bright, very clever. But emotionally, she's really immature. A neglected girl. She's so hungry for love. Like an orphan. She has to know twenty-four hours a day that you love her. (*Coming back to his daughter*) All right, so who's perfect? Apparently, I'm attracted to childish women. Your mother, she should rest in peace, till the day she died she was fifteen years old. (*Sits down again, leans across to his daughter, the pleading naked on his face*) But this girl is sweet, Lillian, I can't tell you. She has such delight in her. Like a baby. (*He looks at her, his eyes wide and beseeching*) Do you think I'm making a fool of myself, Lillian?

THE DAUGHTER

(*Drops her eyes, frowns*)
Well, Pa, it's really not my business to interfere in your life.

THE MANUFACTURER

At least, a few years of happiness I'll have. Even a few years of happiness, you don't throw away.

THE DAUGHTER

I never met the girl, of course . . .
(THE DAUGHTER *scowls, looks away, then stands.*)

THE MANUFACTURER

Your opinion is very important to me, Lillian. I'll be honest with you. I'm not sure of myself in this thing. (THE DAUGHTER *is looking around for her cigarettes again*) Don't go home yet, Lillian.

THE DAUGHTER

I'm just looking for my cigarettes, Pa.
(*Her husband offers his pack; she takes one.*)

THE MANUFACTURER

(*Rising and following her*)
What I'm afraid, you see, is like Walter Lockman needs prostitutes maybe I need a young bride.

THE SON-IN-LAW

(*Standing suddenly*)
Jerry, you love her?

THE MANUFACTURER

(*Turns to his son-in-law*)
Like a schoolboy.

THE SON-IN-LAW

And she loves you? So that's the whole thing. Get married.

THE DAUGHTER

(*Snapping at her husband with rather sudden intensity*)
Sit down and stay out of this. It's none of your business. (THE SON-IN-LAW, *stung a little, shuffles back to his chair.* THE DAUGHTER *turns to her father*) Pa, I'm going to be frank with

you. The relationship, to say the least, seems to be a neurotic one. The girl is obviously infantile in many ways. Otherwise, she wouldn't have to look to older men. I don't know the girl, but obviously she is very dependent, very infantile. And the whole relationship doesn't sound to me like the basis for a sound marriage. It sounds to me more like a father-daughter relationship than a husband-wife. It sounds like you want to adopt her, rather than marry her.

THE SON-IN-LAW

(*Sitting in his chair, without looking up*)
Your father's nobody's fool, Lilly.

THE DAUGHTER

Jack, please . . .

THE SON-IN-LAW

The man wants to get married. All he wants to know is that you're happy for him.

THE DAUGHTER

I don't want him to do something he'll regret the rest of his life. (*There is something familiar about the sentence she has just said that is unpleasant to* THE DAUGHTER *and makes her frown*) I'm just saying, weigh the circumstances.

THE MANUFACTURER

(*Stands but avoids the eyes of the others*)
All right, all right. We discussed it enough. I don't want to talk about it any more. (*He puts the cigar down on an ash tray, crosses slowly to a window, looks out at the heavy snow.* THE SISTER *appears in the anteroom*) I'd go out for a walk, ex-

cept it's snowing so much. I can't stand snow. I wish I was
going to Florida with you. I'd like to go to bed. I'm tired. I'm
usually asleep by this hour. When you get to my age . . .
(*He breaks off, once more aware of his age.*)

THE DAUGHTER

Pa, all I'm trying to say is . . .

THE MANUFACTURER

(*Crying out*)
All right! I don't want to talk any more about it, do you
hear me!
(*He starts up to the anteroom, but his sister's presence
makes him turn, and instead he goes to the chair over
which his jacket is draped, and takes it.*)

THE DAUGHTER

Pa, why don't you come home with Jack and me, don't go
in to work tomorrow, spend a long week end at our house?

THE SISTER

(*As her brother moves into the anteroom to go to the closet*)
Jerry, where are you going? Go to bed, for God's sakes.
What are you going down for, a paper, what?

THE MANUFACTURER

(*Getting his coat out of the closet, mutters*)
Look, leave me alone for a couple of minutes.

THE DAUGHTER

(*Coming to him in the anteroom*)
What did you say, Pa? I didn't hear what you said.

THE MANUFACTURER

(*Turns to his daughter and cries out more in pain than in anger*)

I said, "Leave me alone!"

(*Carrying his coat, he wrenches the door open and exits from the apartment. The door closes heavily behind him.* THE SISTER *lets out a deep sigh and comes down into the living room.*)

THE SISTER

All right, all right, it's not so bad, it's not so bad. He's all upset now. Tomorrow he'll be sulking. In a couple of days he'll be all right, same old Jerry. One thing I know, a man gets to middle age, God alone knows.

THE DAUGHTER

(*Coming down into the living room to her husband, who is standing and glowering at the floor*)

I knew something like this was going to happen. He lives here lonely. His friends have all died or moved to California. Naturally, he's going to . . .

THE SON-IN-LAW

Come on, let's go home.

THE DAUGHTER

(*To her husband, who has walked to the anteroom*)

Listen, Jack, I really don't think I can get away Monday for Florida. My father is going through a very crucial period now, and . . .

THE SON-IN-LAW

(*Slowly bursting out with all the repressed submissiveness of
years. He stares at his wife, the words stumbling out*)
Boy, you're great! Boy, you're great! Sure, the trouble with
Evelyn, she got a neurotic attachment! Holy Jesus Christ!
He came to you, he says he's going to get married, and you
whack him across the face with some two-bit psychology!
Can't go to Florida now! I knew it! I knew it! Your father
needs you! Oh, sure, boy! Your father needs you like a hole
in the head! How many times I heard that? My father needs
me! You need your father, that's what! I knew we weren't
going to Florida! I knew it!

THE DAUGHTER

Jack . . .

THE SON-IN-LAW

You're the one! You! You! Who's all tied up with your
father! Took me two years to get you to move to New
Rochelle! Couldn't live half an hour away from your father!

THE DAUGHTER

Now, listen, Jack . . .

THE SON-IN-LAW

Shut up! I'm talking now! I'm going to Florida, you hear
me?! I don't care whether you come! Everything is for your
father! Three times a week you got to call him on the phone!
I'm your husband, goddammit, you know that? Jesus Christ!
How about me?! I want to go away for a vacation! How about
thinking about me sometimes instead of your goddam father?!

113

(*The shrill, fierce, tortured fury is so new to him that he feels physically sick. He stands, hunched a little, his face forward, his mouth open as if he were retching, his breath coming in the deep, exhausted way of a truly ill man. Then he says quietly, his eyes closed*) I'm sorry, Lillian, I'm sorry. Come on, let's go home.

(*He turns and shuffles to the front door, where he waits. His wife, who is standing, pained and shocked at the outburst, guilty, confused, shamed, now moves slowly to the steps of the living room.*)

THE DAUGHTER

(*Looking at the floor as she goes*)

I didn't know you felt so strongly about my father, Jack. (*She goes up into the anteroom*) Would you like to have a cup of coffee before we start driving? (*Turning to her aunt*) Evelyn, is there any coffee? (*She turns back to her husband*) Jack . . .

THE SON-IN-LAW

(*At the door, looking down*)

Come on, let's go. It's late, and I got to drive the sitter home yet.

(THE SON-IN-LAW *disappears out into the landing.* THE DAUGHTER *frowns, pauses, turns to her aunt.*)

THE DAUGHTER

So, Evelyn, would you call me and let me know what happens?

THE SISTER

Listen, don't worry. You go home with Jack. He's tired and nervous.

THE DAUGHTER

(*Nods nervously*)
So good-bye. Call me if something happens.

THE SISTER

Nothing's going to happen.

THE DAUGHTER

All right, so call me.
(*She goes out, closing the door behind her.* THE SISTER *stands a moment, then turns to pick up the fruit bowl.*)

Curtain

ACT THREE

ACT THREE

Scene 1

No sooner is the stage dark than the lights come up brightly in THE GIRL'S *apartment. It is the same night.* THE MOTHER *and* THE KID SISTER *are seated in the living room, listening to* THE HUSBAND, *a young man in his late twenties, slim, dark, attractive in the diffident fashion of Montgomery Clift. He seems to be a pleasant, controlled young man, and is dressed neatly except for a somewhat flashy collar and necktie. He sits, his cigarette dangling from between two long fingers.*

THE HUSBAND

. . . I look in to see if there's any mail. The clerk says, "There's a special delivery letter for you." So I see it's from Betty, so I open it up. The first sentence is the greatest. "Dear George. I want a divorce."

THE MOTHER

Oh, my God.

THE HUSBAND

"I'm interested in another man. I want a divorce."

THE MOTHER

Oh, my God, I never knew about this, George.

THE HUSBAND

That's the night I called you three o'clock in the morning, New York time.

THE MOTHER

(*To* THE KID SISTER)
Did you know she wrote a letter to George?

THE KID SISTER

No, I didn't know anything, Ma.

THE HUSBAND

(*Suddenly singing effortlessly, improvising tonelessly*)
"Man, I want that woman . . ." (I wrote this one day. I felt so torchy one day, I just noodled with the piano, and it just came out). "Man, I want that woman . . . wahde-oodle-la-da-doo-dee . . . Wherever she may be. My arms, my lips, my body says, 'Baby, come to me.'" Simple little lyric. Mel Torme was out there. I played it for him. He was very excited about it.

(*He stands, moves around gracefully but a little nervously as he looks for an ash tray.*)

THE KID SISTER

There's one right there on the table, George.

THE HUSBAND

(*Finds the ash tray*)
I don't know. I'm beginning to think there's something wrong with women as a class. Don't get me wrong—I like women. I'm okay that way, don't worry about that. I can

hand you a long list of references, believe me. But women, you know, don't seem to have the capacity to just yak it up. The only time Betty was happy was when she was crying. In my limited experience, it seems women like to be hurt. They always seem to love you more after they cry. (*Smiling with great sweetness now*) Betty, you know, sometimes I'd tease her, and she would cry. I don't know. I was just kidding around. But after she cried, she was always so beautiful. I never raised a hand to her, though, I'll tell you that. You're a woman, Mrs. Mueller. Do you agree with me?

THE MOTHER

(*Not sure what he is talking about*)
About what, George?

THE HUSBAND

I like women. Don't get me wrong. But for laughs, men are more fun to be with, don't you think? My mother always used to say that. "You have to break a woman's heart before she's happy." My mother is a tough old lady, I'll tell you that. She tamed my old man pretty fast. Poor bastard.

THE MOTHER

Don't use that kind of language, George.

THE HUSBAND

Oh, I'm sorry, Mrs. Mueller. (*Looking at his watch*) Hey, it's twelve o'clock, you know that?

THE MOTHER

I don't know what time she gets in any more.

THE HUSBAND

How long she been going out with this man?

THE MOTHER

She used to stay out till two, three o'clock in the morning, even when she was in high school. I never knew where she was.

THE HUSBAND

She was a virgin, Mrs. Mueller, when we got married.

THE MOTHER

Oh, thank God for that.

THE HUSBAND

I still don't know what happened that last night. I happened to wake up four o'clock in the morning, she was gone. I look in the bathroom, she ain't there. But who figured a divorce? I figured I forgot her birthday, something like that. Suddenly, I get a letter from out of the blue, she wants a divorce. That hurt, you know? Your wife wants a divorce, the inference is that you failed as her husband. That's a reflection on me as a man. I took quite a kidding around about that. All the guys in the band, you know? "What's the matter, couldn't you keep her happy." I took quite a kidding around.

(THE GIRL *appears on the landing, cannot find her keys, rings the bell.*)

THE MOTHER

She must have forgot her keys.

THE HUSBAND

(*To* THE KID SISTER, *as he puts on his jacket.*)
So I was telling you about Marlene Dietrich. Man, I tell
you, that woman is architectured.

THE KID SISTER

You know who I think is beautiful? Janet Leigh.

THE HUSBAND

Oh, yeah, sure, she's a nice one, that one.
(THE MOTHER *opens the front door.*)

THE GIRL

I forgot my keys, Mother. It's really snowing outside. Did
I wake you up?

THE MOTHER

George is here.

THE GIRL

(*Frowns*)
George? Where, here? (*She lets the door close and moves
quickly through the foyer to the living-room doorway.* THE
HUSBAND *rises from his chair*) Well, for Pete's sakes. Hello,
George, you look just fine . . .

THE HUSBAND

You look great yourself.

123

THE MOTHER

(*Coming in through the living-room doorway*)
He called about ten minutes after you left the house. So I
told him you were on a date, so we were just sitting around
talking, that's all.

THE GIRL

Well, you look just wonderful, all brown. Why don't you sit
down while I hang up my coat. My mother says your mother
says you got a staff job at NBC.
(*She goes back into the foyer, down to the hall closet,
and hangs her wet coat on the outside of the door.* THE
HUSBAND *follows her to the doorway.*)

THE HUSBAND

(*Calls down the foyer to her*)
Well, not exactly. I got a buddy of mine, staff piano man at
NBC, and he says he can get me in, probably one of the
smaller networks. Tony was trying to round up a four-piece
combination for a night club spot in San Francisco. But it
didn't look good to me, and you know me and Lou Waters
never got along.

THE GIRL

(*Coming back up the foyer*)
That was the horn man.

THE HUSBAND

Yeah, some horn man! He couldn't blow his nose, what a
horn man. So Eddie Johnson, he used to play in the pit in the
Roxy before they put in Cinemascope—I think you met him

once—he wrote me, he said there's going to be a spot open on WPAT, that's out in New Jersey, for a good staff piano man with a classical background. So I figured that's steady work, a couple of hundred bucks a week, so I wired Eddie: "See what you can do for me." So I took the plane in. I mean, after I got your letter, you know.

(THE GIRL *has come into the living room and has been listening, leaning against the couch.*)

THE GIRL

How's your mother?

THE HUSBAND

Oh, she's fine. You look great, Betty.
(THE GIRL *sits down on the couch. Her mother and sister are already seated. A silence hangs over the four of them.*)

THE KID SISTER

So what other stars did you see out there, George?

THE HUSBAND

I caught Sinatra one show. He was at the Sands. Lou Rocco dropped in one night, he sat in for me, so I went over to the Sands, catch Sinatra. Man, he was the greatest. He had laryngitis. He couldn't hit anything over middle F. He had to whisper all his songs. But he was up there for an hour and a half. They wouldn't let him off the stage. The greatest, that man, the greatest. (*Again the uneasy silence. He turns to* THE MOTHER) Would you mind very much, Mrs. Mueller, if Betty and I went for a walk?

THE GIRL

I don't want to go for a walk.

THE MOTHER

Go on out for a walk. He isn't going to kill you.

THE GIRL

I got to get up early tomorrow.

THE HUSBAND

I think you owe me a few minutes in private, Betty. After all, you write me a letter, tell me you want a divorce . . .

THE MOTHER

Listen, Alice and I can go in our rooms, and you could talk right here.

THE GIRL

Ma . . .

THE MOTHER

For heaven's sakes . . .

THE GIRL

(*Suddenly*)

There's nothing to talk about because I just want a divorce because I'm getting married.

(*This statement causes a moment's silence.*)

126

THE MOTHER

(*Coldly*)

Who? To him?

THE GIRL

Yes.

(*She stands.*)

THE MOTHER

I'm not going to let you marry a man old enough to be your father. A Jewish man like that. (THE GIRL *moves away, somewhat like an animal at bay, moves out of the room into the foyer.* THE MOTHER *follows her, herself deeply stirred*) You're always telling me I never took an interest in you! In your school, and things like that! Well, all right! All right! I'm taking an interest in you now! I'm not going to let you throw away the rest of your life! I'm your mother! You listen to what I tell you!

(*They are coming down the foyer now, to the front door.*)

THE GIRL

(*Crying out*)

Ma! Leave me alone!

THE MOTHER

I'm only thinking what's good for you! For you!

THE GIRL

(*Screaming*)

Just leave me alone, please! Will you leave me alone!

THE MOTHER

(*In a fury of desperation*)

For God's sakes! (*She turns, not far from tears, and hurries back to the living room, where* THE HUSBAND *and* THE KID SISTER *stand, embarrassed by the short outburst of screaming*) Oh, for God's sakes, everybody in this building must have heard everything going on in this house! Everything. (*She sits down and begins to cry a little.* THE GIRL *remains in the foyer, by the front door, leaning against the wall, trying to control herself.* THE MOTHER, *talks out loud, to no one in particular*) I don't believe in divorce. You make your bed, you lie in it. My husband wrote me sixteen years ago from Canton, Ohio, he said he wanted a divorce. I said, "You made your bed, you lie in it." The whole neighborhood knows about her and her sugar daddy. I'm ashamed to show my face in the street.

(*She cries again, biting her lip, making no effort to shield her face.*)

THE HUSBAND

(*Nervously, after a moment, to* THE KID SISTER)

What did she do, go out? (THE KID SISTER *shrugs. At this moment,* THE GIRL *opens the door and does go out onto the landing. The sound of the door closing is heard by the others*) She looks good, you know? Listen, I think I'll go out and see if I can calm her down.

(*He ambles out into the foyer and down to the front door.*)

THE MOTHER

(*To* THE KID SISTER)

How's your school coming? Are you having any trouble in school?

(THE HUSBAND *opens the door and looks out.* THE GIRL, *standing on the landing, looks briefly up at him.*)

THE HUSBAND

What are you doing out here, come on in the house.

THE GIRL

I don't want to come in the house.

THE HUSBAND

It's cold out here, you want me to get your coat?

THE GIRL

Would you, please? It's hanging right on the closet there.
(THE HUSBAND *reaches over and pulls the wet coat down from the closet door and goes out onto the landing. The door closes behind him. He helps his wife into her coat.*)

THE HUSBAND

You remember Lou Angosino? You met him once. He was the guy from the union came up the house one time. I think he sat at a table once at Birdland once with us. He made a pass at you. He was out in Vegas. He sends his regards.

THE GIRL

George, I'd like to know why you came back. I mean it, really.

THE HUSBAND

What do you mean, why did I come back? I suddenly get a letter from my wife out of the blue, saying she wants a divorce.

THE GIRL

You said on the phone that you wouldn't contest my divorce. I told you I was sending you a letter from my lawyer which you had to sign.

THE HUSBAND

What are we talking about this out here for? Let's go somewheres where we can talk.

THE GIRL

I don't want to go anywheres.

THE HUSBAND

I'll get my coat, we'll go down, we'll have a beer somewheres.

THE GIRL

George, I'm tired. I'm getting divorced, and I'm getting married, and now you turn up, and it's just a little too much for me.

(THE HUSBAND *looks at the dirty tiles of the landing.*)

THE HUSBAND

Listen, the landlord, what's his name, wrote me, wanted to know if we were moving out. What did you do, give him my address?

THE GIRL

What? Yes, I gave him your address.

THE HUSBAND

I sent him a check for two months.

130

THE GIRL

What is it that's so terrible about marrying an older man?
Lots of girls marry older men.

THE HUSBAND

Well, you know.

THE GIRL

You know what?

THE HUSBAND

Well, you figure a girl who's running around with an old
man, he's usually got a lot of dough, and he buys her fur coats.
I'm not saying that's you because I know you're not a bimbo.
But that's the picture you have when you see some beautiful
girl on some old man's arm.

THE GIRL

It was nothing like that.

THE HUSBAND

It's understandable, you know, you've been here alone for
a couple of months, and you know, it's like when guys get
separated from their wives when they're in the army. I used
to know a girl whose husband was in the army. This was
before we got married, I mean. But she was lonely, you know.
It didn't mean she didn't love her husband. But every now and
then, she'd give me a call. It was just a physical thing. I mean,
that's understandable. But I just can't see you with this old
man.

THE GIRL

I'm going in.
(*She rises, starts for the door.*)

THE HUSBAND

I'm only going to be in tonight and tomorrow. I got to fly back tomorrow night. I got two more weeks to fill out in Vegas. Give me twenty minutes, will you?

THE GIRL

(*Looks at him for a moment*)

George, you're just going to make a pass at me. If you want to talk, I'll be glad to. (*Turns to him*) I've thought so much about us. You need a girl who doesn't need you, and I need too much from everybody. We're so wrong for each other, I wonder why we ever got married. (THE HUSBAND *has begun to make a tentative pass at her. She pushes his arm away with annoyance*) Cut it out. That's just what I mean.

THE HUSBAND

Let's go have a beer somewheres.

THE GIRL

(*With slowly graduated anger*)

What do you think, I'm going to go to bed with **you**? What do you think I am?

THE HUSBAND

Take it easy, will you? I flew all the way back here, I had a two-hour layover in Los Angeles, just to see you. I suddenly get a letter out of the blue, my wife wants a divorce. Maybe I'm a little hurt. Maybe you ought to hear my side.

THE GIRL

It took me four days to write that letter so you wouldn't think I was blaming you.

THE HUSBAND

I won't stand in the way of a divorce, if you want it. What the hell, I don't want any wife that don't want me. I didn't know you were so miserable with me. What did I do? I don't know what I did that you say you were so miserable with me. I thought I was a pretty good husband. What did I do? I thought I kept you pretty happy.

THE GIRL

George, what would you do with a woman if you couldn't make a pass at her?

THE HUSBAND

The trouble with you is I've always got to make you cry.

THE GIRL

I'm going in.

THE HUSBAND

(*Now he is trying to embrace her*)
Don't tell me you didn't miss me.

THE GIRL

(*Trying to avoid the embrace*)
I'm going in. I don't feel well.

133

THE HUSBAND

Betty . . .

THE GIRL

I don't feel well.

THE HUSBAND

I missed you so much I used to go crazy.

THE GIRL

I don't feel well.

THE HUSBAND

What did I do wrong, Betty? Whatever I did wrong, I won't do it again.

THE GIRL

I don't feel well.

THE HUSBAND

I swear I won't do it again.
(*He finally manages to kiss her. She responds for a moment, then throws him off violently. She sinks to the floor, sobbing. As he watches her,*

The lights fade slowly

SCENE 2

THE MANUFACTURER'S *apartment, an hour and a half later.
It is now a little after* 1:00 A.M. *The only light is from a reading
lamp in the living room.* THE SISTER *is seated on the soft chair
beneath it, reading a newspaper. She wears a knitted wool
sweater.*

*For a moment, she presents a solitary tableau. Then the
door to the apartment is heard being opened, and* THE MANU-
FACTURER *enters.* THE SISTER *rises but doesn't move to him.* THE
MANUFACTURER *takes off his coat and hat, places them in the
foyer closet. He seems in control of himself.*

THE MANUFACTURER

(*Mumbling*)

It's stopped snowing.

THE SISTER

What did you say, Jerry?

THE MANUFACTURER

(*He closes the closet door and comes down into the living
room*)

I'm so tired I don't even feel like washing myself. I feel
like falling down on the bed with my clothes on and going to
sleep. Lillian and Jack went home?

135

THE SISTER

Yeah, they went about ten minutes after you went out. Listen, the girl called. She called twice actually. She called about twenty minutes after you went out, and she called again about a half an hour ago.

(THE MANUFACTURER *sinks down onto the seat, not visibly affected by this information.*)

THE MANUFACTURER

What did she say? She want me to call her back?

THE SISTER

She just wanted to know if you was in.
(THE MANUFACTURER *glances at his watch.*)

THE MANUFACTURER

It's twenty after one. Do you think I should call her? (*The phone suddenly rings.* THE MANUFACTURER *frowns. He rises and goes to the phone as it rings again. He picks it up. On phone*) Hello? . . . Hello, Betty, how are you? I just came in the house . . . No, no, I just came in the house. I went out for a walk and I just . . . Yes, I told them. Did you tell your family? . . . Well, where are you? . . . It's half-past one, dear. . . . Well, what exactly is the trouble? . . . Oh. When did he come in? (*He listens for a long moment, his eyes closed*) Betty, I think we should both go to sleep and . . . All right, would you like me to come pick you up? . . . Well, where could we meet? I'd ask you up here except my sister . . .

THE SISTER

Ask her, ask her, I'm going to sleep anyway.

THE MANUFACTURER

(*Frowns on phone*)
Do you want to come up here? . . . I'll come and pick you
up . . . I don't want you walking in the streets this hour of
the night . . . All right, grab a cab . . . All right, sweetheart.
(*He hangs up.*)

THE SISTER

What did she want?

THE MANUFACTURER

Her husband is in town.
(*He stands with great weariness.*)

THE SISTER

Do you want me to put up a pot of coffee?

THE MANUFACTURER

Would you, Evelyn? I'd appreciate it a great deal.

THE SISTER

Sure.
(*She starts for the anteroom but pauses when her
brother speaks.*)

137

THE MANUFACTURER

If it'll make you feel any better, Evelyn, I think she wants to call the whole business off. The first thing she says to me on the phone is, "Did you tell your family yet?" Her husband's in town. The whole thing has become so messy. A divorce, a whole messy business. Really, something you could find on page four of the *Daily News*.

(*He moves around the room, hands in pockets, enclosed once again in his quiet, introspective cage of amiability.*)

THE SISTER

Jerry, take off those wet shoes, you're going to catch a good cold. I'll get a towel, you'll wipe your feet. I'll bring you the shawl to put around your legs. It's freezing in here. We haven't had steam since twelve o'clock. I want you to complain tomorrow about that.

(*She starts for the anteroom again.*)

THE MANUFACTURER

(*A little irritated*)

Don't bring me no shawl. I'm not an old man to sit here with a shawl around my legs.

(*But* THE SISTER *has disappeared off into the apartment.* THE MANUFACTURER *continues to move around the room, his brows thick and knitted. Aware he is alone now, he suddenly permits himself the luxury of an animal-like grunt of pain. Then he quickly shakes his head to clear it of its confusion.* THE SISTER *returns with a towel, a heavy, long foot shawl and a fresh pair of socks.* THE MANUFACTURER *regards her balefully.*)

THE SISTER

All right. Just dry your feet and put on a new pair of socks, that's all.

(THE MANUFACTURER *sits down and, with some wheezing, bends to take off his shoes.*)

THE MANUFACTURER

I'll tell you something funny. I knew she was going to call tonight. I had a feeling, when I came in the house, you were going to tell me she called. (*His sister hands him the towel and he begins to dry his feet*) The truth of the matter is, this marriage is not a good idea. I was going to take her to dinner tomorrow and tell her. (*He stands, frowns, assembles his thoughts*) It would be like living in a foreign country and not speaking the language. Expatriates. It won't work. I tell you, I'm amazed how swept away I was by impulse. I was drunk. The whole last couple of months, I was pie-eyed. Drunk with vanity. Drunk with middle age. Well, listen, it was a wonderful experience.

THE SISTER

Jerry, put on these socks.

(*He moves around in his bare feet, scowling.*)

THE MANUFACTURER

I'll remember this girl as one of the sweetest things in my life. But it was candy. I'm too old to eat candy. You can't build a permanent life on candy.

THE SISTER

I told Lillian, "Your father, don't worry about him, he'll come home, he'll be the same sensible Jerry."

(THE MANUFACTURER *walks around, his face drawn now, the pain visible beneath his self-control.*)

THE MANUFACTURER

(*Muttering*)

You know, I love her, Evelyn. What should I tell you, I don't love her? I love her. I'm trying very hard to be sensible about this business, but my head feels like it's going to explode like a bomb. She tells me her husband is at her house. You don't think I'm not jealous? You know what just flashed through my mind right now? Maybe she went to bed with him. You know that makes me feel sick? I feel sick. Why should she call me one-thirty in the morning? Something must have happened there. I said to her, "It's half-past one, for God's sakes." No, she wants to see me right away. (*He throws up his hands*) Have you ever seen me in a state like this? Is there anything more pathetic than a middle-aged man who falls in love? I'll never be sure if she really loves me. I held her in my arms, and she told me she loved me, and even as she was saying the words, I was thinking, "She's caught up in the moment." She called me on the phone five minutes ago. I was very calm. (*Thoroughly agitated*) Calm. My whole stomach fell out. What can she see in me, a man with a paunch, for God's sakes?! A hundred good-looking young fellows will chase her around the block, what can she want from me?! I mean, let's face the facts, for God's sakes! She doesn't love me! All right, she loves me! I'm a nice man, I got a kind heart. But she doesn't love me like . . . I don't know what. It's sweet what we have, but it isn't in the fingers, in the muscles. It isn't love, you know what I mean? It isn't a man and a woman. (*He turns away, almost shaking from his lack of articulateness*) I don't know what! All I know is I'm trembling and I'm nervous. Go make the coffee, will you, Evelyn? I don't like you to see me like this.

THE SISTER

(*Moving a step toward him, with genuine compassion*)
Jerry . . .

THE MANUFACTURER

All right! All right! It's over! I'm going to tell her it's over. (*He looks away, quite upset now, trying to regain his usual control*) It dies hard. Do you know what I mean, Evelyn? (*He turns back to her*) It dies hard. I feel that something inside me is dying right now. You know what it is? (*He stares at her, his face illumined by a stumbling and almost ineffable insight*) I want to be loved by a woman. And that want dies hard. When you give up that want, it's a very painful thing to go through.
(*He furrows his brow and rubs his closed eyes.*)

THE SISTER

Jerry, for heaven's sakes, you're a successful man, you got a fine business, you got . . .

THE MANUFACTURER

I would appreciate being alone right now.

THE SISTER

Listen, Jerry . . .

THE MANUFACTURER

(*Profoundly tired, he is shading his eyes with his hand now*)
Evelyn, I feel lousy, and I would like to just be alone for a
couple of minutes.

THE SISTER

I'll go put on the electric coffee maker.

THE MANUFACTURER

Please.

(THE SISTER *moves off into the apartment, carrying the
shoes and socks.* THE MANUFACTURER *paces around the
room, frowning, grimacing. He finds himself by the
window, looking out into the dark, lightless street. He
stands there a moment, and then he begins to cry,
quietly, unostentatiously. He suddenly feels cold and
rubs his hands. He goes to his chair and sits down
again, hunched within its confines, so that he seems
smaller. His shoulders are drawn together and his arms
are between his knees to protect him against his shivering. He seems older, almost like a little old man. His
eye is caught by the shawl lying on the arm of the
chair, and, frowning, he takes it, unfolds it over his legs,
tucks it in around his feet, and just sits, huddled and
tired and cold. The doorbell chimes.* THE MANUFACTURER
rises quickly, extricating himself from his shawl. For a

moment, he doesn't know whether or not to put on the clean socks, then decides to answer the door in his bare feet. THE GIRL *enters.*)

THE GIRL

Jerry, I just realized it's half-past one and . . .

THE MANUFACTURER

It's all right, it's all right.

THE GIRL

I couldn't sleep. I wanted to see you because 1 need to be near you. I couldn't just stay home alone.

THE MANUFACTURER

It's all right, sweetheart, come in.

THE GIRL

I felt so foolish when I was coming over here. I was going to tell the cab driver to take me back, but I had already told you I was coming and you were waiting for me and . . .

THE MANUFACTURER

Give me your coat, sweetheart.

THE GIRL

(*As he helps her out of her coat*)
How do you feel, Jerry?

THE MANUFACTURER

I'm fine. How do you feel? (THE GIRL, *freed of her coat, moves nervously down into the living room.* THE MANUFACTURER *hangs her coat in the closet*) I have some coffee going in the kitchen.

THE GIRL

I'm confused, very confused, and yet I feel very sure. There are so many things I wanted to tell you before . . . and I never said.

> (*At this moment,* THE SISTER *appears, cautiously curious. She darts a quick glance at* THE GIRL.)

THE SISTER

> (*In a low voice, to her brother*)

Listen, the coffee is on. It'll be ready in a couple of minutes. You'll hear the bell ring.

> (THE GIRL *turns at her voice.*)

THE MANUFACTURER

Evelyn, this is Mrs. Betty Preiss.

THE SISTER

How do you do, pleased to meet you.

THE GIRL

How do you do?
> (*She turns away.*)

THE SISTER

So I'll say good night. I'm going to sleep.

THE MANUFACTURER

Good night, Evelyn.
> (THE GIRL *nods good night.* THE SISTER *exits.* THE MANU-
> FACTURER *closes the closet door and comes down into the
> living room.*)

THE GIRL

Listen to me, Jerry. This much I know. I love you. I told
my husband, maybe there's something wrong with loving an
older man, but any love is better than none. What would I do
if I didn't have you, Jerry? I'd go running around like I
always did all my life, running to the movies, watching television, jumping into bed with someone I don't even like—
I might even marry somebody just so I won't be alone. That's
what I've been doing all my life, just filling in the hours, kill-
ing time, and then go to sleep, and say, "Well I managed to
get through another day." Keeping myself busy so I won't be
alone. Well, life has meaning for me when I'm with you.
That's more than most people have. I wanted you to know
that's how I feel, and I want you more than anything in the
world.

THE MANUFACTURER

(*Muttering*)

Even a few years of happiness you don't throw away. We'll
get married. (*He looks at her as she sits gazing up at him*)
I'll go turn off the percolator before my sister gets up. (*He
moves out into the anteroom, and then disappears quickly into*

the apartment. For a moment, THE GIRL *remains seated. Then she stands and takes a few aimless steps. The off-stage buzzing noise of the percolator stops, and* THE MANUFACTURER *reappears in the anteroom.*) Do you want to go outside? I feel like walking forty blocks in the snow.

(*He goes to the chair and starts to put on his socks.* THE GIRL *moves around the room, comfortably, amiably. He sees the shawl, throws it aside in a rather extravagant gesture. They both laugh.*)

Curtain